The Girl Who Was Clairvoyant

The Girl Who Was Clairvoyant

MIGNON WARNER

PUBLISHED FOR THE CRIME CLUB BY
DOUBLEDAY & COMPANY, INC.
GARDEN CITY, NEW YORK
1982

Library of Congress Cataloging in Publication Data

Warner, Mignon.
The girl who was clairvoyant.

I. Title.
PR6073.A7275G5   1982   823'.914
ISBN 0-385-18362-3
Library of Congress Catalog Card Number 82-45549
Copyright © 1982 by Mignon Warner
All Rights Reserved
Printed in the United States of America
First Edition

Author's Note

The seventy-eight cards in the standard Tarot deck are divided into two packs known as the Major Arcana and the Lesser (or Minor) Arcana. There are twenty-two symbolic picture cards in the Major Arcana while the Lesser Arcana has four suits (Swords, Wands, Cups and Pentacles), each of which contains fourteen cards—the usual pip cards Ace to Ten and court cards King, Queen, Knight and Page.

The interpretation of the cards, either individually or collectively, in the Tarot reading mentioned in this book and the explanations of their various meanings are based on my own personal knowledge and understanding of the Tarot.

The Girl Who Was Clairvoyant

Prologue

Black-faced gulls wheeled and dived, soared heavenwards on the warm currents of air, then wheeled and dived again high above the solitary, white-washed cliff-top cottage, their raucous calls reaching a shrill crescendo as they swiftly dispatched a sleek young crow which sought persistently to join them; but the woman sitting gazing out of the tiny mullioned window across the twinkling bay heard none of it. She was oblivious to everything but the nightmare which had taken over her life. It had been that way for three months. Ever since that night on the cliffs . . .

The window was partly open and a gentle sea-breeze billowed in the filmy net and ran like a ripple across the cretonne flower-print curtains. It was hot; the hottest June day for almost a century; but the woman trembled fitfully as though with the cold. A ball-point pen lay across the first few lines of the letter which she had spent most of the morning trying to compose. Scattered in minute pieces on the bottom of the wicker waste-basket set near her feet was the evidence of two previous attempts. She was becoming very drunk. An empty, cut-glass tumbler and an unlabelled bottle of spirits, a particularly fine old brandy smuggled in from France, formerly taken by her for medicinal purposes only, stood well within reach. But her main problem, the real cause of the shakes, was not the increased amount of drinking she had been doing lately. It was fear. If she were to be honest with herself, she would have to admit that ever since that terrible night on the cliffs she had dreaded this moment; feared that she would have to write the letter. Somehow finding a way of putting into as few words as possible what must be said without saying too much.

As if suddenly aware of the racket the sea-birds and the crow were making, she leaned forward and closed the window. The tiny, overfurnished sitting-room immediately became oppressively hot and stuffy; claustrophobic; and she ran the pudgy forefinger of her trembling right hand quickly round the lower part of her throat where the tied bow on the neckband of her oyster-grey silk blouse seemed suddenly chokingly tight. Taking her hand away, she gazed at the softly muted colours in the mother-of-pearl set in the silver cuff-link at her plump wrist. Two large tears slid slowly down her heavily rouged cheeks. The cuff-links had been a gift from Albert on their first wedding anniversary. He had had a good year, she remembered: the weather had been exceptionally fine and he had made twice the usual number of runs across the Channel to France. And now Albert was gone and she was all alone. A poor defenceless widow with no one to turn to for help.

Her flushed face crumpled in a flood of tears. Why should she be made to pay for someone else's stupid mistakes? She made fists of her hands and pressed them hard against her closed eyes; her full bosom quivered and heaved. It wasn't fair. The girl couldn't be clairvoyant. It was some kind of trick . . . A spiteful, cruel trick to cheat her out of what was rightfully hers.

She was fired with a sudden resolve; her long, bright pink finger-nails clawed up the partly written letter and deposited it in a crumpled ball in the waste-basket. For the moment there was no sign of the tranquillizer-resistant nervous tremors which had bedevilled her since the night of her husband's death. Her tears dried up, tautening the flesh covering her burning, mascara-streaked cheeks. Then, sniffing loudly, she took up the pen again, cleaned its leaky point on a scrap of paper and began to write. Deep down she knew the letter would probably never be mailed; that her putting pen to paper was really little more than a cathartic, a purification of her thoughts and emotions. After all, it was the best part of twenty-five years ago that the prediction was made. Adele Herrmann wouldn't remember silly, giggly little Peggy Baldwin, let alone what she had said about the hermit and the girl who was clairvoyant.

But what if Adele Herrmann did remember?

Slowly, the woman looked up and frowned. Was she really prepared to take that risk? she asked herself. She lowered her gaze to the sheet of notepaper and thought about the hornets' nest which she knew was there waiting to be stirred up. Not just possibly by her letter. Inevitably. *That was if Adele Herrmann remembered her and knew more about the hermit and the girl who was clairvoyant than she had let on all those years ago.*

She laid down the pen and stared at it fearfully. No, the risk was too great. She would wait; try and bluff it out. Writing to Adele Herrmann must be her last resort.

CHAPTER 1

The first hint that there was something special about the delivery of mail which Mr. Tyler was making to The Bungalow that morning was the fact that he was wearing his official peaked cap. Which, thought Mrs. Charles, as she watched the postman hoist his mail-bag onto his left shoulder and then pause to lock the door of the tiny red Royal Mail van, indicated that the envelope in his hand was most probably On Her Majesty's Service. Nothing terribly exciting. A telephone bill—

The clairvoyante's eyes widened and a quizzical expression crossed her face.

Not another communication from the Inland Revenue?

Its avid interest in her financial affairs since some public-spirited person had felt duty-bound to pass on to her local tax officer certain totally false information concerning the number of fee-paying clients who consulted her at her home was really getting beyond a joke. So much for thinking that her last visit to the tax office in Gidding had seen an end to the matter!

It took Mr. Tyler five whole minutes to traverse the short distance between the gate and The Bungalow's front door. Mrs. Charles smiled to herself as the postman paused once, then for a second and third time to scrutinise the envelope in his hand.

The first leaves of autumn fluttered about his ankles, a coppery plane-tree leaf, larger than the rest, raising up and flattening momentarily against his dark blue trouser-leg before being lifted off by a gust of wind and tumbling cartwheel-fashion up the path and onto the porch-mat.

Mrs. Charles watched the postman for a moment or two longer, then moved from the sitting-room window to the hall and waited for him on her front doorstep with a welcoming smile.

"Good-morning, Mr. Tyler," she greeted him a few moments later. "Lovely day."

"Aye," he responded, not looking up and frowning at the letter in his hand. "That it is."

"Something special for me this morning?" she inquired.

"Aye, that it is," he replied. "A real puzzler."

The postman continued to frown at the letter, his property until he chose to relinquish it. And that, sometimes, could take Alf Tyler a very long time indeed, longer if any attempt were made by the addressee to hurry things along.

"There seems to be something troubling you, Mr. Tyler," observed Mrs. Charles, keeping her tone as casual as she could. Negotiations were now at their most delicate and critical stage. An ill-advised comment, the wrong inflection in one's voice and Alf Tyler would suddenly feel an urgent need to talk things over with his superiors rather than to act *"off me own bat,"* as he would undoubtedly put it should that unfortunate situation arise.

"Aye," he said, inclining his head a little to one side and squinting at the woman standing before him as he might a poorly wrapped and illegibly addressed package. "That there is. Bin just about bloomin' everywhere, has this." The letter floated tantalisingly, but only momentarily, in front of Mrs. Charles' eyes. "Scarborough, London, then back up North again." He examined a blurred imprint on the back of the envelope. "Twice it's bin to Scarborough. Posted nigh on four-month ago too." He widened his eyes reprovingly at Mrs. Charles. "You can't hold the Post Office responsible for that delay. If folks won't address their letters proper, then they've just gotta thank their lucky stars that their mail finally gets where it's meant to be going and hasn't long since done a disappearing act."

"It's been many years since I've lived in Scarborough—London too, for that matter," said Mrs. Charles pleasantly. "I've lived here in the village for over ten years. The letter *is* addressed to me?" she asked, trying unsuccessfully to get a glimpse at what was written on the front of the envelope.

"Aye," said the postman, laying the envelope flat against the front of his light-weight grey jacket and spreading out the fingers of his right hand possessively over it.

Alf Tyler was not held to be a malicious man, though some would have interpreted the sudden glint in his eye along those lines. Mrs. Charles read it as a warning that the village postman was even less inclined than usual to be hurried on about his business.

His tone took on a slight note of truculence.

"I don't know that I ought rightly to be delivering this 'ere, anyway. I mean, *I* know that you, namely Mrs. Edwina Charles, are Madame Adele Herrmann the clairvoyante, but the Post-master General don't, do he?" He turned his head on one side and narrowed his eyes at her. "Aye, it's taking a lot on meself delivering this 'ere to you off me own bat. Now if Mr. Forbes was to get to hear about it and put in a complaint to my supe-riors . . ." He pursed his lips and shook his head gravely. Then, with an exaggerated sigh of regret which, despite its over-emphasis, was none the less quite genuine, Alf Tyler lifted the flap on his heavy canvas mail-bag. There was a slight pause. Then he shook his head again. "Aye," he sighed heavily; and the letter disappeared from sight into the depths of the bag. "It's more than me job's worth." He patted down the flap decisively. "I think I'd best pop along the road a-ways to your brother's place and then nobody can point the finger, can they? I've done me job proper and nobody can say as I ain't."

Mrs. Charles did not argue with him. Nor did she ask why the letter should be delivered to her brother when it was apparently intended for her. Alf Tyler was fanatically single-minded about the mail he delivered. The job would be done his way and any disagreement with him on this point would serve only to delay that inevitability.

He touched the peak of his cap, bade the clairvoyante a polite good-morning and then set off back along the path to his van. The return trip took almost as long as the outward one. The mat-ter was obviously worrying Alf Tyler greatly.

It was coming up to lunch-time of that same day when the troublesome piece of mail ultimately reached its final destination.

The clairvoyante's brother, Cyril Forbes, having delivered the missive safely into her hands, inched forward on her sitting-room sofa and watched her with eager, inquisitive eyes.

He was some years younger than she was; a half-brother, sharing the same mother but having a different father. They were nothing alike. Physically, he was small and dark with the hooked Roman nose of one of their shared Italian ancestors on their mother's side; whereas his sister was tall and fair like her handsome Austrian father. Cyril had worked the old music halls as a ventriloquist, then with their demise in the fifties, had become a seaside Punch and Judy entertainer. He still did the occasional children's show—some Punch and, if his arm were twisted really hard, a little magic—usually as a last-minute stand-in when one of the other Punch and Judy men working in his area found himself double-booked or became suddenly indisposed. Most of Cyril's time, however, was devoted to monitoring outer space in readiness for an alien irruption (peaceful, and referred to by him as *The Coming*) and latterly to something which he made sure everyone in the village knew he was keeping securely hidden away under lock and key in the old oast-house on his rambling, run-down farm. Because of the curious, somewhat conical-shaped appearance of oast-houses, the village wags found it amusing to joke and speculate amongst themselves about the possibility of his being engaged out there in the construction of some kind of rocket ship; a fiction which Cyril, who revelled in this form of conjecture about himself, then went to even greater lengths to promote. He was also editor, sole contributor, printer and distributor of a U.F.O. magazine which had a growing readership world-wide. He lived increasingly inside his head; had as little as possible to do with the real world; and was quite harmless.

At length, he widened his eyes at the unopened letter in his sister's hand and said, "Aren't you going to see what's in it, 'Del? If you knew the trouble I had getting it off Alf . . . And he had his cap on," he added with a meaningful look.

Mrs. Charles looked up from the envelope which served as a remarkable testimony to the sheer doggedness of the Post Office to ensure that a letter entrusted to their care should reach its intended destination. (The envelope had been readdressed many times in as many different hands with the successful combination of names and addresses being *Madame Adele Herrmann, c/o Mr. Cyril Forbes the Punch and Judy Man, Little Gidding, Nr. Gidding.*)

"There's something extra special about that letter," Cyril went on. "It's been through far too much to get to you to be anything ordinary. If you ask me, there's a very important reason why it had to reach you, 'Del.'"

His sister gave him a thoughtful look. While Cyril could be most perceptive, it was unusual for him to take the trouble to communicate his opinions. Purely for selfish reasons. An opinion voiced—an unsolicited one at that—indicated a willingness to become involved; and that was not at all like Cyril. Though this sudden burst of normalcy could be an indication that he was about to retreat temporarily further into his shell; become even less communicative; more vague. If that were possible, thought Mrs. Charles, smiling to herself as she slit open the envelope and removed the letter inside. With it was a picture postcard which, for the moment, she placed on one side.

"Alf Tyler was right," she said slowly. "This is dated the best part of four months ago. The fourteenth of June last."

She read from the letter out loud . . .

"Dear Madame,

"I hope you remember me, though I do not expect that you will as it was so long ago, nearly twenty-five years, but perhaps you will remember Mr. Bridger's concert party. I was the fair-haired acrobatic dancer. Peggy Baldwin was my real name, but I used the stage-name of Margo Lee. (I married after the close of the 1957 Summer Season and moved here to this little Cornish seaside village with my husband Albert.) I know you are going to think this is very peculiar, but my reason for getting in touch with you again after all this time is to ask you if you remember

the party that Mr. Bridger gave at the close of that season. You were working on the pier and your brother was putting on Punch and Judy shows on the sands for the children, and so Mr. Bridger invited you both to come along too and join in the fun. I do hope you remember that party because—"

"I remember it," Cyril interrupted. He was sitting with his elbows on his knees; face cupped in his hands. "And her. Peggy Baldwin. Silly as they come. Giggled all the time. You just had to look at her and off she'd go!"

"Yes," said Mrs. Charles, nodding. "I remember her too. Mostly for the same reason, although she was a beautiful dancer." The clairvoyante's dark blue eyes narrowed reflectively. "But she had a weight problem. She was a very highly strung girl and she relieved her nervous tension by overeating. I seem to recall that it cost her a career with the Sadler's Wells."

Cyril nodded, his head still cupped in his hands. He said, "I remember Bridger tearing strips off her that night for eating too much. He said she'd eat herself out of a job if she didn't watch it."

Mrs. Charles looked at him for a moment, then returned to the letter. "Where was I?" she murmured. "Ah yes, here we are . . . Mr. Bridger's end-of-season party."

She skipped a line or two of irrelevancies, then continued to read aloud:

"You looked at the Tarot cards for me and told me that I would soon meet a man from the sea and have a very happy marriage with him. Well, you were right. Two weeks after Mr. Bridger's party I married Albert, a fisherman. Then after you told me that I was going to get married (I am sorry but I cannot remember your exact words), you went on to say that I should beware of the hermit and the girl who is clairvoyant. Something like that. Well, it is strange about that, what you said about the hermit. I never gave your warning a second thought, not once in all the years since that night at Mr. Bridger's party when you read the Tarot for me, and yet this village where I live is supposed to be haunted by a hermit. It only came back to me the

other day. There is this young girl too, the daughter of one of the villagers, and everyone keeps saying she is clairvoyant. There has been ever such a fuss and to-do about her in all the local papers, and there is even talk of some very important psychic scientists coming down from London later in the year to investigate the strange things that have been going on here in the village ever since her mother realised that she was different. I was talking to the girl's mother recently and that was when I suddenly remembered what you said to me all those years ago. So why I am writing to you now is to ask you what your warning meant. You never said, but I think you knew that the hermit and this girl were going to make a whole lot of trouble for me some day. This is beginning to prey on my mind and there is really no one now that I can turn to but you. I have tried to talk this over with a close friend of mine, but I know it is not much use bothering her with my foolish notions. She would only tell me that I am being very childish and that I should put all this superstitious nonsense out of my head. Dorrie will not have it that Pearl Farrow—the girl who is clairvoyant—can really see things the way people say and make sick and crippled people whole again, but I still cannot help worrying about it. You seemed so sure, and I know deep down inside me that you knew I was going to be in serious trouble over Pearl and the hermit. I would be ever so grateful to you, Madame, if you could find a spare moment some time to let me know what you think I should do about all of this. I really am very worried.

> *Yours very sincerely,*
> *Peggy May (née Baldwin).*

P.S. Please give your brother my kind regards. P.M."

Cyril looked at his sister.

"What d'you make of all that?"

"Nothing good," she replied with a faint shrug.

"Can you remember the reading you did for her?"

The clairvoyante was thoughtful for a moment: then, ignoring the question, she looked at the address given at the head of the letter and murmured, "Michaelmas Cove via St. Ives, Cornwall."

She picked up the picture postcard which had been enclosed with the letter and studied it. "'. . . *considered to have some of the finest cliff-walks in England,*'" she said, quoting part of what was printed on its reverse. The pictorial side of the postcard was broken up into six small shots of special scenic interest in the area. One showed a white-washed fisherman's cottage set high on a bleak-looking cliff. There was a smudged cross marked in leaky ball-point in the square the cottage occupied and beside it, in a hasty ink-blobbed scrawl, were the words, *"My cottage."*

"What are you thinking, 'Del?" asked Cyril, watching his sister's face intently. "You're not going all the way down to this Michaelmas-place just to see Peggy about her letter, are you?"

"I fear it's too late for that," she replied absently.

Cyril regarded her thoughtfully. Then, accepting what she had said as a positive statement of fact and one which carried with it a ring of finality which sounded an ominously unequivocal death-knell for Peggy May, he said simply, "Why didn't you tell her what was going to happen to her if she didn't heed your warning?"

"We were interrupted . . . I'm trying to remember by whom." The clairvoyante gave her brother a startled look. "By you, I think."

He shook his head at her questioning look. "It's no use asking me, 'Del. I haven't got your memory. I can't remember. Did I?"

"Yes," she said meditatively. "I'm sure it was you. I remember now. You came up to us and said that someone—a man, I think you said—was at the door asking for her. Peggy jumped up and vanished in the crowd, and that was the last I saw of her. I haven't seen her from that day to this."

"There were a lot of people there that night," Cyril said, leaning back on the sofa and folding his arms across his chest. "I remember that. Quite a few gatecrashers. Bridger was very put out about it."

"Yes," she said, nodding.

"Would you have told her the truth? I mean, if she hadn't disappeared the way she did that night?"

She shook her head quickly. "One has to make what is sometimes a very difficult decision. Is that person, the one for whom you are doing the reading, capable of handling the truth and dealing with it intelligently?"

"She wasn't," said Cyril, sounding very definite about it.

"No," agreed his sister. "Peggy was the type who would've always needed someone stronger to lean on. A man—"

"That reminds me," he interrupted her reminiscently. "Wasn't she the lass they were keeping an eye on? She'd taken an overdose of aspirin or something . . . Boy-friend trouble, I think." He hesitated. "No; perhaps she was depressed about her weight. I forget now. But I'm pretty sure it was her, 'Del. A few of the other girls in Bridger's concert party shared digs with her, and they took it in turns to watch her and see to it that she was never left on her own. Night and day. I *think* it was her, 'Del. But then again—" he shrugged "—you know what my memory is. It could just as easily have been one of the girls in the dancing troupe. Bridger was always going mad about one or another of them and their boy-friend problems. They nearly drove him out of his mind."

Cyril looked at his sister and waited for her to speak. He was not surprised when she said, "I must go to Michaelmas Cove. As soon as possible, Cyril." She smiled faintly. "And while I appreciate how much you're enjoying the pantomime you've been putting on these past few weeks for the villagers' benefit concerning your activities in the oast-house, I think you should join me. Not right away but later on, perhaps. I may need your help with this."

There were a number of things the clairvoyante could have said in addition, not least of which was that she knew it would be foolish of her to think that she could handle the matter on her own. There would be no David Sayer around this time to argue her case: she would be completely alone, in strange, possibly hostile territory. Meddling in other people's affairs was always a risky business; in this instance, she thought uneasily, probably very dangerous. One might say she knew too much: at least one person living in Michaelmas Cove or its environs—someone other than Peggy May, that is—was going to think so, anyway. Set foot in Michaelmas Cove and that person would know why she had come. It would be too much of a coincidence for there to be any other reason for her turning up there . . .

Cyril was speaking.

"What are you worried about, 'Del?" he asked.

"Specifically?" She looked at him; thought for a moment. Then: "The girl who is clairvoyant."

They fell silent. Mrs. Charles thought about what she had just said, while Cyril considered what he should do in regard to the oast-house.

"Do we know anyone in the St. Ives area?" Mrs. Charles asked at length.

"Sandycombe is near St. Ives, isn't it?"

Mrs. Charles got up and went to a large pigeon-hole in the writing bureau and sorted through a bundle of maps for one of the West Country. Finding the one she wanted, she opened it out on the dining-table and pored over it. Then, after a minute or so, she said, "Yes. And Sandycombe is only a few miles distant along the coast—about five, I'd say—from Michaelmas Cove. Michaelmas Cove is between the two; St. Ives and Sandycombe."

She looked up at her brother expectantly.

"Harry the horse," he said. "He lives in Sandycombe." Then, in response to his sister's blank stare: "You remember him. He used to work with The Great Marlene. We were on the same bill on the halls."

"The man who couldn't feel any pain because he was born that way; the professional hypnotic subject? *That* Harry?"

"A *horse*," said Cyril. "That's the proper name for someone like Harry. In the business, that is." Cyril's dark eyes shone. "What a character he was. Marlene could do just what she liked with him and Harry'd never feel a thing," he said with relish. "I've seen Harry do things to his arms and legs with great long needles that'd make your hair stand on end. The Human Pincushion—that's how Harry started out, you know. Before he teamed up with Marlene. In a circus."

"And he lives in Sandycombe?" asked Mrs. Charles, without too much enthusiasm. (Already she was regretting having said she wanted Cyril along.)

"His family does; and that's what I heard Harry did after the halls closed. He went back home. There was all that trouble about hypnotists—the government ban preventing them from performing on-stage—so he and Marlene split up. Marlene went in for mentalism, and Harry got involved with promotional work for trade exhibitions." Cyril was grinning hugely. "Harry had this one particular publicity stunt that was really terrific. He used to let himself be buried alive for days on end in a coffin he carted about with him all over the place; but in the finish he had to give it up. Being buried alive. His family objected: they said it was bad for business."

Mrs. Charles looked at him.

"The Brents . . . Harry's folks," he explained. "They're undertakers."

CHAPTER 2

The distinctive, uniquely American style of hotel management which had so impressed Tony and Liza Murdoch while on their honeymoon in Miami and shortly thereafter been carefully duplicated by them at The Mermaid was a fair reproduction of the original. As close as an English hotel with English proprietors and an all English staff (Cornish—The Mermaid was a Cornish hotel staffed by local people, born and bred, whose hackles rose to a man when anyone called them, or the hotel in which they were employed, English) was likely to get.

Architecturally, of course, The Mermaid was British to the core; nothing like its Miami counterpart. In common with the other three hotels in Michaelmas Cove, it was a conversion; the main building having been constructed during the early years of the reign of Queen Victoria and used as a retreat for young theology students (those, it was rumoured, who had entered the monastery outside Sandycombe and were going through a crisis of faith). With a decline in the number of young men entering the priesthood (or in those suffering nervous breakdowns—if one gave any credence to the rumour about the true purpose of the retreat at Michaelmas Cove), the Church had sold the property to the local district council which had occupied the building until 1968 when it became impossible for its burgeoning administrative departments to be contained under the one relatively small roof. In January of the following year, Tony Murdoch's father, a publican from London's East End, who had always dreamed of owning his own little place somewhere in the West Country, acquired the property at a fraction of its real worth; made a few cautious alterations and renovations; did away with "St. Michael's House," by which name the building was then still known; renamed it The Mermaid and proceeded to run it on much the same Spartan lines as those endured by the young monks of Queen Victoria's day.

The early seventies and the advent of the Spanish package holiday saw Murdoch senior on the verge of bankruptcy and suffering from severe depression. Whereupon he did the sensible thing: he handed over The Mermaid to his more enterprising son (retaining a small interest in it for himself and his wife, and the right to a roof over their heads for life), and promptly took a package holiday on the Costa del Sol to recover his health.

It was a second marriage for both Murdoch junior and his new wife, Liza. They were then in their late thirties; former circus performers (they had spent twenty years touring the Continent with a Spanish circus); had made a lot of money; and unlike Murdoch senior, were not afraid to spend it. They invested heavily in the hotel and persuaded their bank manager to do likewise. Result: deluxe rooms with private bath *en suite,* modernised standard accommodation, colour T.V. in all rooms, entertainment every evening in the lounge/dining-room, a heated swimming-pool (with coy mermaid mosaics decorating the bottom of the pool and its surround), a fun-room for the small fry with Space Invader machines and room service (deluxe accommodation only) providing light snacks until midnight. The staff had balked at saying "Have a nice day" when Liza Murdoch had tried to introduce the Americanism into their workaday vocabulary. However, with their employees otherwise reasonably willing to oblige (and bearing in mind that they could be counted on to be courteous and polite to the guests, anyway), Liza had graciously conceded defeat on this point and agreed with her husband that they should be more concerned with the spirit of the matter rather than the letter.

Liza, when she heard the rumour about the supposed original use of St. Michael's House, had also thought it might be a nice idea to have a friendly resident ghost—a young cowled monk, she decided, who prowled the hotel corridors late at night chanting matins. But all reference to him was surreptitiously withdrawn from The Mermaid's colourful holiday brochures the year after a quick-thinking would-be rapist had protested his innocence and tried to discredit the evidence of the woman who had accused him of accosting her late at night in the corridor outside her room at the hotel, by claiming that she was a hysteric who had confused him with The Mermaid's ghost.

Upon arrival at the hotel, guests with reservations for deluxe accommodation were presented with a carnation (for the ladies) and a book of matches bearing their gold-embossed names. Also an assortment of brochures on the various day-trips available (The Mermaid had its own coach-tour service which operated out of the hotel three times a week); and a clutch of general information leaflets which included a breezy American-style menu of snacks available from room service, and a detachable form on which guests could award by means of a tick or a cross in the appropriate square, their rating for the various facilities and services provided.

Few guests bothered to complete the rating form and hand it in, preferring instead verbally to assure the desk clerk (in response to her customary parting query) that everything had been *v. good*. Which did not surprise the Murdochs. The average British hotel guest rarely complained; not to the right people, anyway. However, while the leisure facilities at The Mermaid arguably deserved an *excellent* rating, the service and food were really rather poor (though no more so than any other British hotel of its type).

Mrs. Charles, when she arrived at The Mermaid early in the afternoon of Monday, October thirteen—three days after she had received Peggy May's letter—was given a large, fluffy pink carnation. The desk clerk, a pretty, friendly girl of seventeen who wore an identity brooch which said, *"Hi, I'm Penny,"* locked up the office in reception and carried Mrs. Charles' luggage to her room. The chef, the female cleaning staff and the two girls who shared shifts on the reception desk were the only permanent staff kept on all year-round; and in the low season, the reception clerks' duties quadrupled to include porterage, some light housekeeping duties and room service—an arrangement which worked remarkably well until a guest chose laundry-time mid-morning to check out or to ask for his car keys. When that happened, the chef (eventually) ascended the basement-kitchen steps, unlocked the office and attended to the needs of the (by then) usually rather testy guest.

The permanent staff accepted their low season work-load with a minimum of grumbling; particularly Penny who had only recently started at The Mermaid and knew when she was well off. Out of the total number of boys and girls in her class, only six had found work on leaving school. The rest went straight onto the dole. For some it would never be any different.

As for the proprietors themselves, during the low season, Murdoch junior tended bar, waited at table and was in every way the genial and cordial Mine Host referred to in The Mermaid's holiday brochures; while his wife assisted the chef, pined for the carefree days of the circus, and moaned incessantly to all and sundry about her mother-in-law's persistent refusal to vacate the small sitting-room in the Murdochs' shared private family suite when the younger Murdochs finished up for the day.

Penny left Mrs. Charles' suitcase on the luggage-rack near the door, quickly checked that there were fresh towels, et cetera, in the bathroom, and was gone before Mrs. Charles had time to turn round and thank her.

Mrs. Charles got a glass of water from the bathroom for her carnation; and then, attracted by a hollow "thwumping" sound and women's voices, she went to the window and was not surprised to find that her room overlooked the swimming-pool. A lumpy, late middle-aged woman in a black one-piece bathing costume was sitting on a loafer watching another woman swim the length of the pool and back again. The sun was shining brightly but there was a sharp edge to the breeze which rippled the surface of the clear blue water and stirred in the fallen leaves scattered over the aqua-tiled pool-surround. The woman on the loafer seemed unconcerned by the chill to the early autumn day: there was not even the palest tinge of blue to her bare flesh. Mrs. Charles admired the woman's fortitude (or determination—she wasn't sure which was more appropriate in the circumstances), then shivered involuntarily as the swimmer finally left the water.

Leaving the carnation on the sill, Mrs. Charles turned away from the window and unpacked the few things she had brought with her. When she had finished, she glanced through the brochures and leaflets she had been given; noted mealtimes and the polite request that she settle her bill for the week tomorrow, Tuesday (she couldn't remember ever having encountered this before in a British hotel); smiled over the rating form (thought it rather negative of the proprietors to suggest in this way that their hotel was anything other than the very best), then decided to get straight down to business. More hollow thwumping accompanied by the high-pitched voices of young children put paid to any ideas she might have had of resting after her trip down to Cornwall, which had been a long and complicated one. Coach from Gidding to London, a rugby scrum on London's crowded underground railway system, train to St. Ives, then coach again.

A short while later, she went out. As she made her way through the reception hall, she paused to read the printed posters pinned to the notice-board. On Wednesday, Thursday and Friday nights the local amateur dramatic society was putting on a farce at the Village Hall in the Old Quarter; and Sandycombe's annual soap-box derby was being held on Sunday afternoon. The soap-box derby might just do the trick, she thought, making a mental note to introduce some mention of the event casually into the conversation when she phoned her brother (who was procrastinating about joining her; doing his best to wriggle out of it). Worth a try.

Moving on past the fruit machine and the pay phone to the desk, she paused again to inquire about places of interest in the immediate vicinity which could be comfortably visited on foot. Penny said there should be a number of brochures of the sort Mrs. Charles required, including a very interesting one all about the Old Quarter (as she spoke, Penny leaned across the counter and quickly searched through some glossy coloured leaflets in a wall-rack to the left of the desk); but unfortunately they appeared to be out of them. She promised to have a look round the office later on when she had a free moment. There was bound to be one for the Old Quarter lying about somewhere, she assured Mrs. Charles with a smile.

Mrs. Charles thanked her and, on turning to leave, found herself confronted by the frankly amused gaze of the grey-haired woman who had come in quietly from the street while Penny was going through the leaflets. The woman, who was uncommonly tall for a female, five feet nine inches, was dressed for walking in a bold hound's-tooth check suit and flat-heeled, lace-up shoes. Smiling at Mrs. Charles, she stepped up to the desk and said, "You don't want to take any notice of that tourist claptrap, m'dear." Her voice was bluff; deep and masculine. "They've missed out all the best bits. Which was probably their intention, wouldn't you say?" she asked Penny.

Penny contrived to look put out; laughed lightly. "You'll be giving us a bad name, Mrs. Claythorpe, and frighten all our guests away."

The quick look Penny gave Mrs. Charles and the manner in which she spoke conveyed the impression that Mrs. Claythorpe might be a bit of an embarrassment; someone to be humoured but got rid of as quickly and politely as possible. Penny lowered her gaze onto something on the shelf under the counter on her side of the desk and busied herself with it; as if in the hope that when she looked up again, Mrs. Claythorpe, having received no further encouragement from her, would have disappeared.

Mrs. Claythorpe watched the girl and smiled to herself. My God, they were a funny lot. But at least she understood them; what made them tick. That was half the fun of living in Michaelmas Cove . . . Prodding them and their sacred cows with sharp-pointed sticks!

Never one to miss out on an opportunity for some sport, the old lady chuckled throatily and said, "Not got a weak stomach, have you, m'dear?"

Penny's head shot up, but Mrs. Claythorpe was neither looking at nor speaking to her.

"No, of course not," Mrs. Claythorpe went on, smiling again

at Mrs. Charles and making a bet with herself that Penny was holding her breath. "You're not the type. A woman after my own heart; no nonsense and get on with it. I spotted that the moment I laid eyes on you."

"If you mean, am I easily frightened by stories of ghosts?" said Mrs. Charles, smiling back at her, "then the answer is no."

"Ghosts?" Mrs. Claythorpe smote her thigh with her leather gloves and roared with laughter. "The only ghosts—ghost—we've got is real. Isn't that so, Penny?" she asked the now very embarrassed girl on the desk.

Mrs. Claythorpe smiled to herself as Penny glanced quickly down the hall . . . No doubt making sure that silly, paranoid Murdoch-twit was nowhere about the place; Liza Murdoch being such a connoisseur of the art of telling a good ghost story!

"Take no notice of Mrs. Claythorpe," Penny advised Mrs. Charles. A smile flickered half-heartedly on the girl's lips. "I've never seen any ghost. Nor to my knowledge has anyone else in Michaelmas Cove."

"That's only because you're all such a lazy lot," retorted Mrs. Claythorpe. "You spend as much time as I do walking on the cliffs and then we'll hear what you have to say."

"You've actually seen the hermit, have you?" Mrs. Charles asked her.

Mrs. Claythorpe looked at her; smiled. "Good for you, my girl," she said. Then, with a sly wink at Penny: "The hermit indeed! Methinks we've got a believer here." She looked back at Mrs. Charles. "We must have a good long chat some time." Her tone was faintly mocking and she looked both amused and vaguely pleased about something. This, thought the clairvoyante, is all for Penny's benefit. Mrs. Claythorpe was deliberately teasing her. But it was not a personal matter; something strictly between the older woman and the younger one. The girl, Mrs. Charles suspected, merely symbolised something which Mrs. Claythorpe took pleasure in goading.

Mrs. Claythorpe, looking back at Penny, smiled and said, "I guess I'd better tell you why I called in . . . Mrs. Bastian asked me to stop by and let you know that Deanna won't be in tomorrow. Deanna's come down with the flu—or something of the sort —and her mother thinks she had better stay in bed out of the cold."

Penny looked concerned. "Can you give me some idea how long she'll be off work? So that I can tell Mrs. Murdoch. She'll want to know."

"I haven't a clue," replied Mrs. Claythorpe. "If you like, I'll ask and drop in again tomorrow afternoon on my way out for my walk and let you know." She turned to Mrs. Charles. "Perhaps we'll meet again; have that chat then."

She waved an arm in the air and was gone. The heavy glass vestibule door swung to behind her. It was spattered with large raindrops even though the sun was still shining brightly.

"She seems a very lively old lady," observed Mrs. Charles with a smile.

Penny looked at her; then gazed pensively through the door which gave onto the small vestibule. "Mrs. Claythorpe really should know better. She doesn't look it, but she's well over seventy and she forgets that she's not as agile as she used to be. Some of the paths over the cliffs are particularly treacherous in this kind of weather. It's so changeable at this time of year; clear and fine one minute and damp and misty the next. You weren't thinking of taking a walk on the cliffs too, were you?"

The sudden, wide-eyed look Penny fixed on Mrs. Charles made the clairvoyante feel as old as Methuselah.

Mrs. Charles said no; she proposed to take the short bus-ride into Sandycombe and spend the afternoon there looking at the shops.

Penny watched her leave. The girl looked upset about something and was, in fact, quite worried. Dee hadn't said anything to her that morning about feeling off colour. Though there had been something wrong. She hadn't done any of her rooms properly. Towels missing from one; no toilet paper in another; the wastebasket unemptied somewhere else. And she had completely missed doing anything at all to the bathroom in fourteen.

Penny's uneasiness increased. Maybe it had something to do with last night. Dee went white as a sheet when the glass spelt out that message. She swore it didn't mean anything to her, but it did; you could tell by the look on her face and the quick way she denied knowing what it meant. Penny chewed the corner of her bottom lip. She wished she hadn't taken part. It was all Josie's doing. She kept on and on about trying to get in touch with her uncle Albert. Penny's flesh crawled at the remembrance. They were a weird lot, the Mays. She'd never felt really comfortable with any of them. Josie wasn't too bad—sometimes; but as for her uncle Albert and that brother of hers, Felix . . . What on earth had Dee seen in him? *Yuk!*

Penny stopped chewing her lip and her expression became intensely thoughtful. Josie hadn't liked it when Dee had finished with Felix. She had never actually said anything, but there was something odd about the way she would look at Dee sometimes; something really creepy. As if she really hated her for what she had done to Felix and was just waiting her chance to get even with her. The Mays were a very close-knit family. There was a lot of talk about them behind their backs, but nobody dared openly cross them. And they never let anybody get the better of them. Nobody that she could think of. Except Dee.

Had Josie fixed it in some way for the glass to spell out that message?

Penny considered the possibility.

She didn't think so. Her finger had been on the glass too, and she couldn't recall being aware of anyone *forcing* the glass in any one particular direction. If anything it had seemed to float around the ouija board— S-C-A-R; then, when Dee said the word *scar* meant nothing to her and Josie suggested they should try again in case there was more to the message, E-D. S-C-A-R-E-D. *Scared!*

And Dee had been scared. Really scared. She'd sat there frozen to the spot. And then when Josie'd called her "chicken" for refusing to continue with the game, Dee had put her finger back on the glass with theirs and it had spelt out W-A-T-E-R and then D-E-A-T-H. And that *had* made sense. To all three of them since Dee had nearly drowned once in a swimming-pool accident during a school outing they had all gone on. Josie had said the message was a warning and that Dee should watch out; and Dee had just sat and stared at her; never said a word.

Penny frowned and felt even worse; guilty, because the more she thought about it the more likely it seemed to her that Josie had been deliberately out to frighten Dee. Josie knew as well as she did that Dee had funny moods sometimes and was the kind who took everything to heart and let things depress her. Josie would've known how upset Dee would be about a message like that.

Oh God, thought Penny anxiously. Something dreadful was going to happen. She just knew it! And it would be all Josie's fault. And hers. She would be as much to blame for not having at least tried to make Josie stop.

Deep in thought, Penny locked up the office and went to find Liza Murdoch to tell her that the girl who cleaned the deluxe rooms would be off sick for a few days. With flu, please God, Penny prayed. Nothing more.

CHAPTER 3

As Mrs. Charles came out of the vestibule and descended the green terrazzo steps to the forecourt, a woman appeared in one of the wide lounge windows and removed a black and white sign which read, *"Welcome I.P.R. Members."* This being Monday, it seemed reasonable to suppose that the guests so welcomed had departed the previous day. Mrs. Charles did not need to speculate about the initials: they stood for the Institute of Psychical Research; a woolly-minded bunch of individuals who thought the height of psychical experience was the ability to bend spoons and stop watches and clocks.

The clairvoyante and the institute had fallen out with one another many years ago. As a charter committee member of the I.P.R., it had been a distressing time for the clairvoyante, all the more so since she had been wrongfully accused by one of the other committee members, who was intensely jealous of her, of passing certain "secret" information to a rival institution and she had had to take recourse to the law to clear her name. The institute was not large enough to hold a convention, so she surmised that the members had been holding one of their week-end seminars at The Mermaid. And it was not hard to guess what had prompted them to choose Michaelmas Cove as a venue. In fact it was predictable that they would come. Sooner or later. She debated whether they were the important London psychic scientists whom Peggy May had referred to in her letter. If so, the clairvoyante wryly hoped the girl who was clairvoyant was good at spoons!

The woman was still in the window. She was tall, well built, and had wide Slovak cheek-bones and dark brown eyes. With the exception of the two small curls of hair which had been teased out over her ears like fluffy ear-muffs, her shoulder-length blond hair was drawn back severely on all sides of her face and secured at the nape of her neck in a tortoise-shell clasp. The donkey-brown two-piece knitted suit she wore was expensive. So was her jewellery. And she was wearing a lot of it, the clairvoyante noted. On her fingers—almost, but not quite, as many diamond rings as the clairvoyante herself was wearing. It crossed Mrs. Charles' mind that again like herself, the woman in the window might once have been with a circus. It was what many circus folk did with their money; invested it in valuable pieces of jewellery which they collected obsessively. (The clairvoyante had, anyway.) The woman was also heavily made-up, particularly around the eyes and mouth. Like an actress. (Or a circus performer, the clairvoyante thought, smiling to herself.) Somebody who had grown accustomed to wearing heavy theatrical make-up for long periods of time and now felt stripped completely naked without it.

The woman glanced disinterestedly at Mrs. Charles and turned quickly to Penny who had come up behind her and then moved round to stand with her in the window. Penny spoke to her; the woman's colour rose as she said something in reply; Penny shrugged. Then, abruptly, the woman walked off and Penny, after a moment or two's hesitation, drifted aimlessly away. Penny didn't look any happier than the woman had.

Mrs. Charles paused and stood looking back over her shoulder at the empty window. She felt suddenly very cold, chilled to the bone. The sounds of the street and the colours of the day became muted; dulled. Death was all around her.

The bus journey into Sandycombe was pleasant and took an hour.

The route was farther inland than Mrs. Charles had expected—she had rather hoped that the bus would take the road which followed the coastline round to Sandycombe. In the height of the tourist season, traffic on the rambling Michaelmas Cove/Sandycombe bus-route was bumper-to-bumper. Today, the narrow hilly road was clear, with not a caravan in sight. Even the vil-

lages they passed through were quiet and, in all but two instances, virtually deserted.

Few people boarded the bus en route and there were only two
minor traffic delays; one at a red traffic light in a little village
whose main through road was so narrow it could cope with traffic
only one way at a time (the village bobby—the thinnest, tallest
man Mrs. Charles had ever seen—on his pre-War bicycle was
coming the other way); and the second, a small unattended herd
of dairy cows which had the ancient right to graze on the village
common. With full udders, they were meandering casually back
home through the heart of another tiny village as was their cus-
tom every afternoon at milking-time.

Rain started to fall as Mrs. Charles alighted from the bus at
the Sandycombe pier, which she hoped would be open to the
public out-of-season. It was; though nobody seemed to be using it
at the moment. The fortune-teller's booth, she discovered, was
closed. She could see that the boards were up without having to
pay to go through the turnstile which gave onto the pier proper;
but she paid up anyway.

"Got your anchor with you?" inquired the old man on the
turnstile as his arthritic fingers grappled awkwardly with the
small coins she gave him and he let her pass through.

She looked back at him questioningly.

"Wind's gettin' up. You could get blown away out there in the
open," he warned her, not very seriously.

"Oh, yes," she replied, smiling. "I see what you mean. I'll take
care."

"There's nothing much open at this time of year," he told her
apologetically. He thought she was a very attractive woman;
rather too well dressed for afternoon tea at the pier tea-rooms.
One of the posh five-star hotels along the promenade, like The
Crown, he thought, would be more to her liking. He raised one
of his badly crippled hands and made circular waving motions
with it at the frail-looking glass-domed structure which housed
the tea-rooms, the amusement arcade, the fortune-telling booth
and, of course, the Winter Garden where the summer variety

shows were staged. "Just the tea-rooms and the amusement arcade over there, that's all," he said.

"I was hoping to see the fortune-teller," she confessed, turning back to face him.

"He's closed for the season," the man said. (Blimey, he thought. That was a turn-up for the books. He'd never have picked her for the type who'd go in for that sort of thing!) "Won't be open till Easter. You've a bit of a wait," he said with a cheerful grin. "That's if you're planning on hanging around till then."

She smiled. "No, I don't think so. He?" she inquired.

He nodded. "Old stager, like me," he said. "He's been here for years. Practically part of the furniture."

"Does he live locally?"

"Over in Michaelmas Cove. 'Bout four, five miles along the coast. You'll find him in the Old Quarter; Frenchman's Lane. Ranjat Singh, that's his name. One of them Indian swami fellers. Wears white pyjamas and a bath towel round his head. Everybody knows old Ranji. You just ask; somebody'll soon tell you the way."

"I will," she said. "Thank you."

She moved round and went through the exit gate.

"You're not going on the pier after all?" he asked, surprised.

"No, I don't think so. Like you said, it's a bit windy . . ."

"I can't give you your money back."

"No, I daresay you can't," she said, and smiled.

From somewhere close at hand came the sudden, unnerving sound of shattering glass and she looked back quickly over her shoulder at the glass-domed structure.

"Just the roof," said the old man imperturbably. "Happens all the time when it rains. The panes of glass fall in. Summer, winter; makes no difference. Nuisance in summer when we're busy. They've got to keep turfing everyone out while the council's men clamber up onto the roof and fit new sheets."

The clairvoyante looked at the tea-rooms but there was no sign of the staff, or anyone else for that matter, evacuating the building. The people who worked in the tea-rooms were obviously as blasé about falling panes of roofing-glass as the man on the turnstile was.

"It sounds dangerous," she remarked.

"That all depends on where you happen to be sitting or standing," he said. "Otherwise it's no problem at all."

As Mrs. Charles moved from the protection of the covered turnstile, the wind whipped open her wheat-coloured cloak and she quickly hugged it close to her. The rain had slackened off, but the sky over the rising, muddy-looking sea was black and threatening; and it was growing cold. By the time she had reached the exit from the pier, it was raining heavily again and she took refuge in the narrow, canopied doorway of a charity shop for the mentally handicapped. The shop was closed; and the one next to it, a local arts and crafts centre, and the one after that where during the summer months, a glass-bender sat in the window and made glass animals and birds for the tourists to buy.

The last shop in the row, a confectioner's, was open. A child stood with her back to the clairvoyante in the shelter of its doorway waiting for the rain to stop. She had a wide halo of naturally bouffant, bright ginger hair; so transparently fine and fluffy that it could almost have been spun around her head like candy floss; and she wore a heavy black overcoat which was too long for her, almost to her ankles.

The rain began to ease off and Mrs. Charles moved swiftly from the shelter of one shop doorway to the next. The child looked up quickly as Mrs. Charles joined her outside the confectioner's. Only it wasn't a child. It was a woman of indeterminate age; not really fat and yet peculiarly barrel-shaped in a child's pale yellow cotton daisy-print smock which, like her coat, was much too long. Her feet were so tiny, the rest of her oddly shaped body so ungainly, that she looked in imminent danger of toppling over. She was wearing nothing on her face but a quizzical expression; the kind of look which said, "Don't I know you?"

The clairvoyante certainly knew her. But for the moment she couldn't remember from where or when. The woman's unusual shape finally provided the clue which gave her the answer. Pantomime. She had played the part of Tweedledee in the West End panto in which Cyril had had a small spot with his Punch and Judy.

Mrs. Charles smiled and said, "Tweedledee, Christmas 1972." She remembered the year of the pantomime very well, and with good reason. She was in London at the time to divorce Charles the Third, the last of her three husbands.

The little woman gave a hop and skip of pure delight and launched straight into her pantomime role, with full actions and a kaleidoscope of bizarre facial expressions quoting from her lines which were in rhymed couplets; quite absurd and largely nonsensical.

Mrs. Charles complimented her on her memory.

"I was the witch in *Babes in the Wood* last year," said Tweedledee, and with lightning speed changed into the wicked witch of that year's panto and danced about the rain-puddled confectioner's forecourt like a woman possessed.

A late middle-aged couple walking past stared hard at her.

"I don't care what *they* think," Tweedledee told the clairvoyante loudly, shooting the man and woman a venomous look, and continued with her performance. Eventually she ran out of breath, clutched at her midriff; made a face—and she had a remarkable repertoire of them.

"I've got this pain," she announced abruptly. "Just here—" She grabbed a handful of her smock, drew it out towards the clairvoyante and smacked her lips together as if she had overeaten and was now regretting it. "It comes and goes," she said. "Nerves. That's what this friend of mine in London told me. She lays her hands on my head like this—" Tweedledee showed Mrs. Charles where and how "—and then, *massage-rub-massage-rub*," she crooned. "The pain simply *melts* away," she assured Mrs. Charles with a fierce look. She switched expressions and voices; closed her eyes; spoke dreamily. "I feel as light as a feather; as if I could float-float-float away."

She held her short arms aloft and twirled slowly round and round; eyes still closed.

"A spirit healer?" inquired Mrs. Charles when Tweedledee

(the clairvoyante still couldn't remember the woman's name—she doubted that she had ever known it) spun to a halt.

"That's right," said Tweedledee. "A clairvoyante really, but she also does spirit healing on Tuesday nights. At her home in Wimbledon, just around the corner from my digs. She told me that I've got nothing to worry about. It's just nerves. I think too much about myself, she said."

"Have you seen a doctor?" asked Mrs. Charles.

Tweedledee looked as if she had just swallowed a large dose of nasty-tasting medicine. She shook her head quickly. "It's only nerves; my friend said so." Tweedledee was beginning to look as though she were deeply regretting having met up with this face from the past.

"Your friend is most probably right; but all the same you should also see a doctor. Have you been going to her for long?" inquired the clairvoyante.

"I've only been twice. I'm going again as soon as I go back home. She's *marvellous!*" Tweedledee rubbed her midriff; grimaced. "I'd give *anything* for a session with her right now." She made some more lip-smacking noises; looked vaguely around her.

"Spirit healing and clairvoyance are greatly underrated—" Mrs. Charles began cautiously. Tweedledee did not appear to remember that she was a clairvoyante and Mrs. Charles saw little point in reminding her. Tweedledee had made it perfectly plain that she would only ever hear what she wanted to hear. And that did not include the proviso (another warning to seek orthodox medical advice) which the clairvoyante was about to add.

Intuitively foreseeing the direction Mrs. Charles was taking, Tweedledee neatly cut her off by dramatically clapping her small hands together and whirling round once. "*I knew it!*" she said in a stagy squeak. "I took one look at your face and I said to myself, 'She's got it; that same look Hilda has about her!' You have, haven't you? Tell me I'm wrong! You've got the gift too." Her eyes narrowed and she crouched forward with her hands held up at head height and shaped like animals' claws. "You don't read the cards, do you?"

"Yes, as a matter of fact I do." Mrs. Charles wondered if Tweedledee had actually finally remembered that she was a clairvoyante or whether she was merely latching onto the first thing which came into her head and using it as a diversionary tactic. The latter seemed the more likely of the two.

"You haven't got them with you, I don't suppose?" Tweedledee said challengingly.

Mrs. Charles shook her her head regretfully.

"Pity," said Tweedledee with some more lip-smacking noises and looking vaguely about her again.

"Are you working at the moment?" asked Mrs. Charles.

Tweedledee shook her head and said she had been on the dole since *Babes* closed in March. She made a fierce face and shook a clenched fist at Mrs. Charles. "*'You little madam!'* I say to myself every time I pick up my social security cheque. 'You should be ashamed of yourself. Go out and get a job in a canteen or something.' I'm a Cordon Bleu cook," she said, which surprised Mrs. Charles who would not have thought she could reach the top of a stove let alone put something on it to cook. Tweedledee glanced into the confectioner's. "I was hoping they'd have a copy of *The Stage;* but they don't sell papers. I wrote off for auditions for all of this year's pantos, but I couldn't get anything. I'm answering all the singing and dancing ads at the moment hoping for something there." She made another face. "My dancing's okay—" she did a bit of tap to prove it (she was actually wearing black, flat-heeled tap-dancing shoes minus the special tapped heels and toes) "—but I've still got some work to do on my voice. I'm having lessons."

She didn't sing, but she puffed out her egg-shaped chest and projected her voice to show how she was making out in that direction.

She clutched at the front of her smock again; smacked her lips together; looked vaguely up and down the street. "I shouldn't have drunk that Coke with my fish and chips at lunch-time," she said wistfully. "That's where I'm staying; over there." She pointed at a small guest-house across the road. "I'm waiting for a friend. He'll be down in a day or two and then I'm going to have a couple of days' holiday here with him before moving on to Manchester and Edinburgh." She spoke as if both places were just around the corner in the next cove, not some hundreds of miles distant. "We really must meet and have a good long chat sometime." Tweedledee put the suggestion to the clairvoyante the way some people do on parting; those who have absolutely no intention of seeing the person to whom they are speaking ever again. Not if they can possibly avoid it.

"I hope you find something soon; a job," said Mrs. Charles. "And do see a doctor about that pain."

Tweedledee held out her coat like the wings of a giant bat and twirled and whirled round and round away from the clairvoyante, faster and faster, across the wide pavement to the pedestrian crossing.

Rumpelstiltskin, thought the clairvoyante with a smile. One more twirl and she'd vanish in a puff of smoke!

A bus was coming, its lights shining weakly in a fine misty drizzle. The one for Michaelmas Cove, the clairvoyante hoped, moving swiftly to cross the road and hail it.

The return trip took longer than usual due to the worsening weather conditions. Visibility was poor, and as the bus turned onto the wet, jet-black strip of road which ran along the sea front at Michaelmas Cove, it appeared that some disaster had recently taken place, either on the quay or somewhere close at hand. The Sandycombe Fire Brigade had been called out and an ambulance was standing by.

The two middle-aged women sitting together on the seat in front of Mrs. Charles squirmed round as they drove past the quay and stared at the scene.

"Somebody must've gone over the cliffs again," one said to the other.

"That's Ida Claythorpe, isn't it?" the second woman said quickly. "There in that carry-chair . . . Coming down the cliff-path between those two ambulance-men."

The first woman looked.

"There ought to be a law," she said disapprovingly. She didn't say against what, but she appeared to have her companion's whole-hearted support for the proposal. That was if the expression on the second woman's face were anything to go by.

"She won't be told," said the second woman.

"No," said the other one. "You might just as well save your breath for cooling your porridge . . ."

CHAPTER 4

There was a grubby, dog-eared brochure suggesting interesting places to visit in Michaelmas Cove waiting for Mrs. Charles under her cup and saucer when she came down to breakfast next morning.

She perused the tiny map of the Old Quarter, looking for Frenchman's Lane, while she finished her second cup of coffee.

Half an hour later, she went out. Reception was deserted; but as she reached out to open the vestibule door, Penny's head and shoulders suddenly appeared round the lounge doorway. The desk clerk called quickly to her.

"You weren't thinking of going walking on the cliffs, were you?" Penny inquired, her tone somewhat apologetic, as if some kind of trespass were being considered and she was both reluctant and embarrassed at having to be the one to point out to the wrongdoer that she was about to walk on the grass.

"No," replied the clairvoyante. She let go of the door handle and turned slowly back. "I thought I'd explore the village and the Old Quarter first, seeing as how you were so kind as to find that brochure for me."

"Oh—" Penny faltered; coloured a little. "It was no trouble." She seemed hesitant about something. Then, coming right into the hall: "I thought you might be heading for the cliffs and I just wanted to warn you to be careful. I wouldn't want you to spend your week with us confined to your room. The lady who called in yesterday afternoon—Mrs. Claythorpe—had a nasty accident up there a short while after we were talking to her."

"She hasn't been seriously hurt, I hope," said Mrs. Charles.

"No, I don't think so. She was very lucky. It's just her leg and an ankle, but to be on the safe side, they kept her in hospital overnight under observation. They thought at first that her ankle might be broken, but it's only a bad sprain."

"I think I might've seen her being taken off by ambulance as I was coming back on the bus from Sandycombe late yesterday afternoon," said Mrs. Charles.

"Probably," said Penny. "You be careful," she added.

Mrs. Charles assured her that she would wait for much better weather before tackling the cliff-walks.

It was overcast but mild. Mild enough for one hardy soul to be out of bed at 6:30 A.M. and in the swimming-pool splashing about! Everything smelled salty-fresh and clean after yesterday's rain. The sea was calm but a muddy-brown colour again as if there were some turbulence going on beneath its unruffled surface.

It was still a little early to go visiting so Mrs. Charles took a leisurely stroll along the sea front. There were not many people about; a few visitors, like herself, killing time—faces she recognised from the coach-party of senior citizens from Kent who had arrived at The Mermaid late the previous afternoon. She saw a postman and was tempted to make inquiries of him regarding Ranjat Singh the fortune-teller, but decided against it. Her own personal experience of this kind of introverted, close-knit community was that it was often quite amazing who reported what and to whom (village menfolk being, if anything, worse gossips and carriers of malicious tittle-tattle than the women); and there was time enough, she mused wryly, for her adversary to find out that she had arrived and was snooping around Michaelmas Cove.

She paused momentarily to take in the view. To her left was the sea; some way ahead of her, the quay and the craggy cliffs—the latter, in the absence of the sun, heavily shadowed and faintly menacing; behind her The Mermaid; to the right of her, the occasional guest-house, some large old Victorian houses which had been converted into self-catering holiday flatlets, an estate agent's and a small unlicenced hotel. Immediately ahead of her, veering to the right and up a steep rise, was the Old Quarter, a rabbit-warren of narrow, cobbled lanes where wooden-beamed drinking taverns (some of which were now gift shops where one might buy the work of local artists and potters) and quaint old fishermen's cottages huddled conspiratorially together, their secrets as safe today as they were back in the days when Michaelmas Cove was a smugglers' haven.

Mrs. Charles spent an hour exploring the Old Quarter, coming at length to an old-fashioned grocer's shop on the corner of Lamppost Lane and another short, unnamed lane which she suspected might be the one she wanted. She was about to enter the grocer's to make her inquiries concerning the whereabouts of Frenchman's Lane and the fortune-teller who lived there when the house name on a door painted in deep red gloss enamel caught her eye. She studied it thoughtfully, then turning away from the shop, she crossed the lane and paused before a brightly polished brass lion's head door-knocker. Above it was a brass number (7), over which was the house name, Nirvana.

The clairvoyante raised the heavy door-knocker and let it fall. She could hear shuffling footsteps on the other side of the door, a pause (she couldn't see a peep-hole but suspected that there was one somewhere), and then the door finally opened.

Mrs. Charles gazed at the bronzed, deeply lined features of the stout old gentleman facing her, at his snowy-white turban with its amethyst-blue jewelled adornment, and a slow smile spread across her face. "Why Courtney Harrington. You old reprobate! Indian swami indeed!"

"Bless my soul!" responded the old man, wide-eyed. "Well, bless me if it isn't 'Del Herrmann! Why this is wonderful, a marvellous surprise."

The man making a mail-order delivery to the terraced house next door was staring openly at them and so the swami quickly put his hands together, prayer-fashion, backed away from the door, bowing profusely from the waist, and begged his visitor to enter his humble home.

With the door safely closed behind them, he reaffirmed his pleasure at seeing the clairvoyante.

"My goodness me," he went on wonderingly. "It must be all of fifteen years. How's that brother of yours? Still got his head in the clouds?"

Mrs. Charles smiled. "I'm afraid so."

"Good for him!" said the swami heartily. "Half his luck . . ." He sighed. "To be so happy and contented, not giving a damn for what people think." The troubled look which stole across his face was replaced by a quick smile. "Come through and sit down," he urged, leading the way into his small, fern-filled front room. A joss-stick burned in a corner, heavily scenting the air with its distinctive fragrance. "How did you find me?" he asked, motioning to the sofa.

"Purely by chance," she replied, sitting down. "I was expecting to find an Indian gentleman. I had no idea that Courtney Harrington and he were one and the same person," she confessed with a smile.

His bright blue eyes twinkled. "I hit upon the swami gimmick some years ago—shortly before I came down here to Cornwall to live. I'd been going through a bad patch and I felt that what was really needed to set matters to rights was more than just a change of address. I needed a whole new personality; a completely different approach. So I opened up a little place on the pier at Sandycombe, just a bit along the coast; and for a time things certainly did take a definite turn for the better. And then—" He broke off, shaking his head. "Well, you know how it is, 'Del. Life's old see-saw. Up one minute, down the next. I had hoped to settle here permanently in Michaelmas Cove: I was even negotiating to buy a small fisherman's cottage up on the cliffs for my retirement. I had it all worked out. Another couple of years at Sandycombe and that would be it; I'd close up shop there and settle down for good in my little white-washed cottage and grow pelargoniums. Business was booming— It always is when times are hard." He paused and made a small gesture with his hand. "People finding themselves suddenly faced with problems they've never had to cope with before; worried about tomorrow; looking for the quick cure for all that ails them; the simple solution . . ." He sighed. "I won't say they were queuing up to see me, but it wasn't far off it. And then instead of minding my own business, I made the cardinal mistake of calling another clairvoyant a fake."

"Pearl Farrow?"

He laughed quickly; bitterly. "Even you've heard about her!"

"A little." Mrs. Charles paused and looked at the swami thoughtfully. "Well, Courtney," she said. "Is she, the girl who is clairvoyant, a fake?"

The swami sighed again, then swept the turban from his head and placed it on the ornately carved occasional table between his visitor and himself. Leaning back in his chair, he stroked his hand across his shiny bald pate and then down over a narrow semicircle of downy white hair to the back of his neck. He left his hand there for a moment, then raised his shoulders a fraction and said, "No. She's the genuine article all right."

He looked at his visitor; frowned. "I was so sure of it, 'Del. *Positive.* Pearl Farrow *had* to be a fake. All the predictions she was making, the miracles—or at least, those attributed to her, worked in her name—were nothing but inspired guesses; coincidence. Or worse . . . In the case of the predictions, she'd already looked at the answers long before the questions had been asked."

His mouth set hard and straight and he shook his head slowly. "No way! Once in a lifetime somebody like Pearl Farrow comes along, 'Del, and the pity of it is that it had to be in *my* lifetime and on *my* patch. If only I'd kept my mouth shut and let her get on with it. But no; I had to be clever. My pride had been pricked. Anything Pearl Farrow could do, I could do better. Only I couldn't. And do you know why, 'Del? The reason has been staring me in the face for years, but I refused to see it. I am a good all-round fortune-teller, but I lack inspiration—divine inspiration, if you like . . . That special something which has set you, and Pearl Farrow, apart from the rest of us. I've always admired you tremendously, 'Del," he confessed morosely. "Aye, and there was even a time when I was jealous of you and your gift."

"I know, Courtney," she said softly. "But I think you grossly underestimate yourself. One can only be inspired if all the signs are favourable." She smiled a little. "We can all be apocalyptic in the right set of circumstances."

He smiled back at her affectionately. "You've got a good, generous nature, 'Del. You always did have." His tone became wistful. "Aye, and perhaps there lies the answer. You would've accepted the girl for what she was and never have made the complete ass of yourself over her that I did. I was so desperately determined to prove that she was a fake—" he sighed "—and all I achieved was the loss of my own credibility. Who would believe a word old Ranji had to say after all the terrible things he said about Pearl Farrow? Half the folk here won't even speak to me any more!"

Mrs. Charles looked at him contemplatively. "One way or another this girl certainly seems to have had a profound effect on the inhabitants of Michaelmas Cove," she observed.

He laughed dryly. "You suddenly, out of the blue, have a miraculous vision about an old priest, a man loved and venerated by everyone who lives in Michaelmas Cove, and see what effect *you* have on people!"

"Ah," said the clairvoyante, nodding. "So that was it."

"You didn't know?" The swami looked surprised. He folded his arms; frowned meditatively. "It all began very late one night up on the cliffs. We've got some quite spectacular ones, as you'll no doubt have observed for yourself. Caves, too, tucked away about half-way up the cliff-face. The caves are reputed to be inaccessible by land and therefore ideal for getting rid of anything likely to cause embarrassment if found in your possession," he added with a look which, if it were intended to be meaningful, as the clairvoyante suspected, conveyed absolutely nothing whatsoever to her that was pertinent to their present conversation. "However," he went on, "to get back to the night in question. Fr. Michael Thomas, the local Roman Catholic priest, was up there late this particular night visiting a sick parishioner and on his way back, in almost total darkness, he missed his footing and went clean overboard. Now at the precise moment he fell, Pearl Farrow—who lives alone with her mother, Mary, in a small cottage at the foot of the cliffs—woke up screaming. Apparently she'd had some kind of dream—a vision—and in this vision she had seen Fr. Thomas falling down the cliffs. She could even pinpoint the exact spot where he fell which meant the rescue team were able to make straight for him. He was found lying on a ledge below Jupiter's Lookout; right where Pearl had told them they would find him."

"How old is the girl?"

"Seventeen; eighteen. Thereabouts." The swami smiled at the pensive look on his visitor's face. "I think I can guess what you're thinking. It was the first thought that entered my head too. Pearl Farrow saw the old boy fall; she was up there at Jupiter's Lookout that night—a recognised trysting-place for young lovers —meeting a boy-friend on the sly; wouldn't dare admit to her mother what she'd really been up to; and so she simply sneaked back home and concocted a story about having been asleep and dreaming that Fr. Thomas had had an accident. Being a Catholic, the idea of a vision probably came easily to her. I thought so, anyway." He shook his head. "Not so. Pearl wasn't out that night. She was in bed seriously ill with a severe chill; feverish. Somewhere around eleven, the fever worsened and Mary—the girl's mother—got a neighbour to come in and sit with Pearl while she came down into the village to fetch the doctor.

"Ah, I can see you thinking to yourself—" The swami wagged a forefinger at Mrs. Charles. "If it wasn't the girl who concocted the story, it must've been the mother." He shook his head again. "Most unlikely. Pearl was far too ill to be left on her own even for a few moments. She's prone to these chills and fevers; has fits when the fever's really bad. Somebody has to be with her all the time. Anyway, the doctor was out when Mary reached her home, so the doctor's housekeeper invited Mary in to wait. And there Mary remained cooling her heels under the housekeeper's watchful gaze until the doctor got back ten to fifteen minutes later. Mary had thought it best to wait for the doctor. You can't get a motor vehicle up to her cottage and there was a power failure that night: all the lamps dotted along the cliff-paths were out between ten-thirty and midnight, and the doctor—a young woman who hadn't been here long—was going to need a guide. Mary's a bit like Michael Thomas—the father; knows those cliff-paths like the back of her hand. It was soon after Mary and the doctor reached Mary's cottage that Pearl, who was semi-delirious by this time, suddenly came to and started jabbering about Fr. Thomas.

The doctor couldn't make head or tail of what the girl was saying but Mary could. Near enough, anyway. Mary had seen Fr. Thomas going past her cottage earlier in the evening, so she knew that he had gone up the cliffs, but she had no idea whether he had come back down again. And, of course, she was away from the cottage between eleven and eleven forty-five fetching the doctor, so she had no way of knowing if anybody had gone past during that time. The neighbour didn't know either: she was too busy keeping an eye on Pearl.

"However, to cut a long story short, the doctor promised Mary that she would phone the priory the moment she got back to the village to make sure that Fr. Thomas had returned safely that night: the prior, when she contacted him some time later said he hadn't seen the old boy since early that evening; and after phoning the sick parishioner's home where Fr. Thomas had been visiting and verifying that he had been gone for quite some while, the prior called the police and they, in turn, called out the cliff rescue team."

The swami hesitated; seemed distressed. Then, with a quick shake of the head: "If only I hadn't been so jealous—frightened, I suppose, of the girl and the threat I felt she posed to me as a clairvoyant myself and had sat down and thought the whole thing out sensibly and unemotionally." He paused and gazed intently at his visitor. "You see, 'Del, Pearl has always been a bit strange; different. Well—" he made a small, dismissive gesture with his hand "—her mother's odd—a harmless, God-fearing woman, but definitely funny in the head—and Pearl's father, apparently, wasn't any too bright. Farrow fell into a wheat silo and was suffocated to death when Pearl, they say, was only a babe in arms. Pearl didn't get much schooling. Her mother deliberately kept her at home on the pretext that the child was sickly, but the truth of the matter is that she realised that Pearl was backward and she wasn't having her mixing with other children where her mental deficiency would be highlighted. (Or so I've heard it said.) Consequently, Pearl never played with the other village children, and apart from the very rare occasions on which she did attend school, accompanying her mother to Mass on Sundays

and to the local shops was as far as she was ever permitted to
venture. Even now, today, Pearl is never seen away from home
without her mother. Mary is very protective towards her; watches
over her like a hawk. And neither one of them ever leaves the village."

He leaned forward earnestly. "You see what I'm driving at,
don't you, 'Del? This sort of thing couldn't have happened to
anybody *but* someone like Pearl." His eyebrows rose signifi-
cantly. "The simple, devoutly religious peasant girl singled
out down through the ages, as she has been, and later canonized
by the Church for their divine revelations and the miracles
they've worked."

The clairvoyante's eyes widened. "Michaelmas Cove another
Lourdes? Is that what you're saying?"

"I don't see why not. For months now they've been coming
every Sunday by the coach-load; the halt and the lame; from far
and wide. Bringing their gifts of money and flowers which they
leave at the shrine Mary Farrow's had erected outside her cottage. That, incidentally, is as near as she'll let anyone get to
Pearl. I'll give Mary her due: she's not turned the girl into a
money-making side-show like some would've done; won't let anyone else do it either. It's all done very decorously and with true
religious regard. They come in silence, kneel and pray at the
shrine in silence, leave their gifts—or nothing at all (Mary has
never asked for a penny from anyone; not that type; fiercely
proud and independent)—and then they leave in silence. People
whose last and only hope is a divine miracle. It's a deeply emotional experience, both for the pilgrims and for anyone witness-
ing the scene. One can't help but be sincerely moved by it all;
and in my case, deeply humbled and shamed."

CHAPTER 5

Mrs. Charles nodded slowly. Then, after a thoughtful pause:

"Jupiter is the Latin for hierophant or priest, isn't it?"

The swami said he believed so. He went on:

"There's an old local legend about a religious hermit, a member of a French order of monks. Bogus apparently. It was a front for a smuggling ring. The fathers on the other side of the water—the 'French Connection,' so to speak—trod the grapes (a rather fine old brandy) and smuggled it over here in small casks, and Bro. Dominic—the hermit of the legend and the 'English Connection'—received the illicit goods and distributed same. As a matter of fact, it's more than mere legend. It actually happened; somewhere in the late seventeen hundreds, I believe. Bro. Dominic is still supposed to skulk about the cliff-paths, keeping a lookout for the King's men and watching for the boats from France. A lot of people claim to have seen him up there in all his ghostly glory."

"Yes, I think I might've met one of them," said Mrs. Charles. "Only this particular lady maintains that the ghost is real."

"Oh, you must mean Ida Claythorpe." He nodded quickly, smiling. "The hermit she saw probably was real. Fr. Thomas again. He's a monk of sorts; and, as I've said, this used to be his parish. He often wore a long brown habit of the type one would imagine the religious hermit of the legend wearing, and he was forever wandering about the cliffs. A close friend of his used to live up there in one of the old fishermen's cottages. Both gone now." He paused and chuckled. "Damn near buried together too. Poor old Michael Thomas was so drunk at the graveside—he officiated at his friend's funeral—that he stumbled and toppled over into the grave onto the casket. The funeral had to be delayed for more than an hour while the mourners sobered him up."

"Dear me," murmured Mrs. Charles. "How very distressing for the deceased's family."

"Well, yes and no. Fr. Thomas was parish priest here for more years than most folk would care to remember. That was point one in his favour. Point two . . . He was raised here. That strengthened the bond between him and the villagers and did remarkable things for their capacity for forgiveness and understanding. He was one of them, not just their parish priest, and was looked upon as being a good friend to everyone in the village, regardless of their faith. And as for his behaviour at his friend's funeral; he'd never been any different. You could always count on Michael Thomas to liven things up, even a wake! What a zest for life that man had. It seems almost criminal to shut him away from the rest of the world."

"I understood you to imply that he too is now dead."

"As good as. After the fiasco at Albert May's funeral . . . well, the Church had to step in and do something about him. He'd been getting progressively worse." The swami's eyes widened expressively. "The drink. His health—liver—was packing up. Nowadays he just lives quietly in the priory on the outskirts of Sandycombe. He comes into the village every so often to see some of his old friends. It was for his own good. If the Church hadn't retired him when it did, he's bound to have walked off the cliffs again one dark night, not knowing where he was or what he was doing. You'll never convince me he hadn't been drinking the night he went overboard. Maybe it even saved his life." He grinned. "He was probably so heavily anaesthetized with alcohol that he landed on the ledge like a limp rag doll. He fell over fifteen feet, and all he got was a mild concussion and a few bumps and bruises."

The swami was quiet for a moment, thinking. "That was something else Pearl told the police—through her mother, of course. Fr. Thomas was alive, she said: she could hear him moaning where he lay." He shook his head; frowned. "In the weeks which immediately followed her vision, Michaelmas Cove

—and Sandycombe, for that matter—were gripped by what to my way of thinking is best described as an emotional hysteria bordering on acute religious fervour. You would be utterly amazed at what has come to be attributed to Pearl Farrow and her powers of second sight. Anything and everything from why the buses have suddenly started running on time to what has caused local hens to lay a preponderance of double-yolked eggs! In short, we've gone from the sublime to the ridiculous. And I blame not the Farrows for all of this nonsense, but the local news media—the *Sandycombe Express* in particular. They really went to town. Mary Farrow, I heard, was very upset about it. She refused to have anything to do with them and threatened to make an official complaint to the police if they didn't leave her and Pearl alone. Which only served to throw more fuel on the fire. It's all settled down now, of course, but for a while there it was getting quite out of hand."

He paused and looked thoughtfully at his visitor. Then, with a solemn smile: "I'm wondering why you should be so interested in all of this—" He held up a hand as Mrs. Charles went to speak. "No," he said, "don't bother to deny it. You're interested all right, or I'm not worth my salt as a clairvoyant." The smile on his face faded. "What are you doing here, 'Del? What has brought you to Michaelmas Cove? It's Pearl Farrow, isn't it?"

A small smile flitted across the clairvoyante's face. "On the fourteenth of June last, someone whom Cyril and I knew a long while ago wrote to me from here—Michaelmas Cove—referring to a reading of the Tarot which I had once done for her. The reading in question was incomplete: we were disturbed half-way through it; and so this woman, who was quite young—a mere girl at the time—only ever got half a prediction. A certain set of circumstances which I would suspect occurred sometime prior to her writing to me made it imperative for her to know what else was in the reading. But unfortunately, due to her addressing her letter to me incorrectly, it took some four months to reach me."

"Who is she, this woman?"

"The widow of the deceased gentleman you referred to a few minutes ago. The priest's friend."

"Albert—" The swami broke off. Then, with a sharp intake of breath: *"Not Peggy May?"* He stared at her for a moment, a shocked look on his face. "Good Lord, 'Del! This is awful; dreadful. The poor woman is dead. She chucked herself off the cliffs; jumped from Jupiter's Lookout—where Michael Thomas went overboard. Only she wasn't so lucky. She missed the ledge and went the full distance; all the way down to the rocks below. Somewhere about the end of June, beginning of July. Terrible business. Peggy and her husband were very close and when he passed on, she couldn't face up to life without him; got more and more depressed; and then finally it all became too much for her. What a pity her letter to you was delayed in the post. If anyone could've set her thinking straight it would've been you, 'Del."

He paused. Then, after a moment, he nodded slowly. "You know all this, don't you? You knew before you came here that Peggy May was dead. I think her suicide was in the unfinished part of the reading you did for her. And something else too. Yes," he said, watching the clairvoyante's eyes closely. "Definitely something else."

She smiled at the thoughtful expression on his face.

"You be careful, 'Del," he said.

"That's the second warning I've had today," she said, still smiling; and in response to his quick frown: "The first related to a walk it was assumed that I was about to take on the cliffs. I'm told they're very dangerous at this time of year."

"Treacherous," he said decisively.

Mrs. Charles looked at him meditatively. "Mrs. Claythorpe had an accident while she was out walking up there yesterday afternoon."

"She's not been badly hurt, has she?" he asked quickly.

"I gather not."

He looked inordinately relieved, as if he had in some way been personally responsible for the old lady's accident and had only just realised it himself. "The silly old biddy! She's nearly eighty, y'know. She simply will *not* be told! The paths over the cliffs should be closed to the public once the season ends. We have a cliff rescue team stationed here during the summer months—a voluntary one made up of young students mostly who are fully qualified climbers and properly trained in that sort of rescue operation. But during winter, anybody who goes overboard has to wait for a rescue team made up of men from the Sandycombe Fire Brigade to get over here; and you don't need me to tell you what a delay like that could mean to someone of Ida Claythorpe's age. I'll pop out and see her in a little while. She lives just over the way—" He waved a hand in the air. "Next door to the grocer's. We foreigners must stick together," he said, smiling. Then, by way of explanation: "Ida Claythorpe and I; we're English. And to paraphrase the wise old saying, 'Cornish is Cornish and English is English, and never the twain shall meet.'"

The smile slowly disappeared. "Up until a few months ago I would've argued with anybody that there was no place on earth like Michaelmas Cove. Nothing would've tempted me to leave; and yet now I can't get away from here fast enough. Everything has gone sour and rotten, and I know that while I remain here I'll have nothing but bad luck. You're sensitive to these things, 'Del. You tell me if there's not something bad here."

The clairvoyante nodded. "There *is* something wrong here, Courtney, but don't turn your back on it and try to run away from it. If you do, the bad luck you fear will follow you wherever you go and for the rest of your life."

He regarded her gravely. He was surprised that she hadn't perceived his situation a little more keenly. Yes, he wanted to run away all right. But he couldn't. He'd dug himself into this mess and only a miracle now could save him from sinking even farther into the mire and being swallowed whole by it.

Deanna—Dee her friends called her—slipped her hand under her pillow and withdrew her black leather-bound diary; opened it at the calendar in the front; found the right month and that day's date, the fourteenth. Then she counted the weeks again. The answer was still the same. She was four days overdue. *Four whole days late!*

She went hot all over.

What was she going to do?

Her mother never asked each month if she'd had a period; she simply checked the contents of the packet of sanitary napkins in the top left-hand drawer of the dressing-table; made sure they had been used up. Dee had watched her doing it. So that was the first thing she would have to do, thought the girl, her heart fluttering against her rib cage. She'd have to remember to keep emptying the packet, bit by bit.

Throwing back the covers, she got quickly out of bed and went over to the dressing-table; paused; stared at herself in the mirror. There were dark circles round her eyes, and she was drained of all colour. She certainly looked ill; quite ill, in fact. Her mother thought so, anyway; and for the time being this was all that mattered. She simply *couldn't* go back to work until she'd seen Ronnie. He'd know what to do. She had told him that she had never done anything like this before, and he had promised her that he would take care of her if anything happened. Nothing *would* happen, he'd said. Nobody got pregnant doing it just the once . . .

Except me, thought Dee miserably.

A wave of nausea rose in her and she felt giddy. She clutched the edge of the dressing-table for support; then, as the sick feeling passed, looked anxiously at the old-fashioned alarm clock on the mantelshelf. Still only five and twenty past eleven. She had at least another hour to wait before she could start getting ready. Ronnie'd be in at twelve-thirty, regular as clockwork. And while her mum was busy giving him her order, she'd slip down the back stairs and out the side door; go straight to the car park down by the quay. Where Ronnie always left his car . . .

She moved to the window and gazed through the net curtain at the bright red door across the lane. The last time she had looked out, something like forty-five minutes ago, old Ranji had been standing on his doorstep talking to a woman—nobody Dee knew; a visitor to Michaelmas Cove. He used to have a lot of visitors, the girl recalled; women *and* men; but not so many people called to see him these days. Not since he'd been so nasty and spiteful about Pearl Farrow. Mrs. Claythorpe was about the only person that Dee could think of who bothered much with the old man. A social outcast, her dad called old Ranji. A fool to himself . . .

Hot tears sprung into Dee's eyes, and her chin puckered and quivered. That was what her dad would call her when he found out she'd been mucking about with a man. A fool to herself. Her heart palpitated and her cheeks burned. He'd go mad; he'd kill her when she told him. And Ronnie. He'd never liked Ronnie much. Al Capone, he called him. Sometimes, the Pied Piper . . . This was when some of her girl-friends would deliberately come into the shop at lunch-time when they knew that Ronnie would be there and start showing off in front of him. Her dad said men like Ronnie had silly little girls all over the country dancing to their tune. That sexy voice of his, her dad said, was the same bait the Pied Piper used on the rats.

Dee frowned a little. Her dad thought he was being very funny; a right comedian. (Was he teasing her because he knew that she secretly fancied Ronnie?) There was something strange about Ronnie's voice, though. It was so very soft—almost musical —and yet strong and commanding. Ronnie just had to ask and she'd do anything for him. She couldn't help herself. It was like being under a spell . . .

The girl drew back quickly from the curtain. Ranji's visitor was leaving.

Dee suddenly found herself wanting to cry. She wished it was her down there with the old man. She wanted to run downstairs and across the lane into his funny-smelling front parlour and sit with him and play draughts like she sometimes used to when she was a little girl. It was so peaceful and quiet in there. Like being in an empty church on a hot summer's day. No shop-bell ringing at all hours of the day and night; no raised voices, her mother complaining about how tired she felt all the time and how nobody cared; no heavy tread on the stairs late at night after her father had been out drinking with his mates. The row that always followed . . .

Ranji glanced her way, but she knew that he couldn't see her. Then he turned and went indoors.

Dee moved back to the window. She had very nearly knocked

on Ranji's door yesterday lunch-time on her way home from work. She had wanted to ask him about the ouija board; if it really could predict things the way Josie said. She wouldn't have told him anything about Ronnie. Or the baby that was on the way. Dee went hot and cold at the thought. Ranji was sure to tell her mother: it wasn't like he was a priest or a doctor, was it? Fortune-tellers weren't under any sacred oath; they didn't count! Her mum would go spare if she found out that she'd been playing around with a ouija board. After what happened to that other girl over in Sandycombe . . .

Dee began to cry. Very softly. What were all her friends going to say when they found out? Penny? Josie? Josie'd say something vicious and cruel. Maybe even laugh at her. And she was sure to start up again about Ronnie being married. Well, he *wasn't* married. He was once, a long time ago, but not now. He'd told her so himself.

Dee felt crushed; bitter and frustrated. Tears flowed freely down her cheeks.

Josie could deny it as much as she liked but she was no different; she'd be in today, a couple of minutes after Ronnie showed up. You just wait and see if she wasn't!

Dee stood momentarily naked as she slipped her pink nylon night-dress over her head and dropped it onto the bed. She caught a glimpse of herself in the mirror as she went to the top left-hand drawer of the dressing-table for a clean pair of panties.

She was nauseated.

Her breasts looked positively *enormous*.

Her mother said it was the first place it showed.

The man turned into Lamppost Lane and started to walk briskly up it, slowing his stride, as everyone was inevitably forced to, when its steep gradient began to take its toll on the backs of his legs. There was no true footpath; just a kerb roughly thirty centimetres wide which ran parallel with the terraced stone cottages lining both sides of the lane. He disappeared into the grocer's shop at the corner of Frenchman's Lane.

Agnes Bastian looked up expectantly as the bell on the door

tinkled and the man came in. Her shiny, short blond hair had been recently brushed and combed and she had put a dab of perfume behind each ear. The man smiled to himself as he caught a faint whiff of it. Nice, he thought. The look he gave the forty-two-year-old shopkeeper was frankly appraising. He liked Mrs. Bastian; she was his kind of woman; a little on the plump side with plenty of boob; the fluffy, feminine type. And if there hadn't been so much other talent about to choose from, she'd certainly have been in with a chance . . .

"Hullo, Ronnie," said Mrs. Bastian with a self-conscious smile. "On time as usual."

The man grinned, laid his brief-case and hat on the counter, then unzipped the brief-case and got out his order-book.

"That's a nice perfume you're wearing today, Mrs. B.," he said smoothly. He stopped what he was doing and smiled; let his pale blue eyes linger on her face; watched her blush.

"Oh," she said quickly, and put her hands momentarily to her face in an affected gesture. "You surprise me. I put it on ages ago—this morning, before breakfast."

Naughty, naughty, he thought, smiling to himself at the lie.

The bell on the door tinkled again and an attractive, dark-haired girl of about eighteen in a chunky black polo-neck sweater, a blue kilt and high-heeled black suede boots came into the shop. She looked at the man coolly; made no attempt to speak to anyone.

"Hullo, Josie," the man said. "You're looking very beautiful today. On your way to work?"

She moved up to the counter; leaned against it looking at him.

"Don't mind me," she said, glancing at Mrs. Bastian. "I'm in no hurry. I'm not due at The Mermaid until five today."

"That gives us a whole four and a half hours," said the man. "What shall we do? Run away and elope?"

Josie flicked her eyes over him, then turned lazily to Mrs. Bastian and said casually, "How's Dee today? Penny rang last night in a bit of a flap and said Dee was sick. She seemed quite worried about her."

Mrs. Bastian frowned. "It's only a sniffle, that's all," she said impatiently. "She'll be back at work in a day or two."

Josie looked back at the man. "Oh," she said. Then, after a slight pause and still watching the man: "Good. I'll tell Mrs. Murdoch."

"We're going to be some time here," said Mrs. Bastian abruptly. "If there's something you want, Josie?"

The girl bought a pack of chewing gum, asked Mrs. Bastian to give Dee her love and to tell her to get better quickly, and then went to the door.

"The King's Head in half an hour," the man called after her.

"You'll be lucky, grandad," the girl replied, going out.

"Saucy young madam," said Mrs. Bastian crossly.

And dangerous, thought the man. A real little minx; so sharp she'd cut herself one of these days. And him too, if he didn't watch out. She'd spotted him last month with Dee up on the cliffs. She hadn't tumbled yet to what was really going on, but perhaps it was time he was moving on. All good things had to come to an end sometime; and he'd been offered that new area nearer to home with much better prospects for promotion. Cut and run, Ronnie, he advised himself. While you still can. Liz certainly wouldn't be sorry to see the back of him . . .

He turned back to Mrs. Bastian and caught her looking at his scar. He suddenly realised he didn't mind. Not any more. Quite a few people now—and not all of them female—had told him it made him look a bit like Jack Palance, the film star. Kind of scary but not ugly. As a matter of fact, he personally had always thought Jack Palance was rather good-looking.

When he left the shop twenty minutes later, his nostrils full of the French perfume which he knew Agnes Bastian was wearing solely for his benefit, he was carrying his hat. Time to get rid of his neurotic inhibitions about his face once and for all. He could forget all about the accident now; the months of pain while they remade his face. All that was behind him.

He smiled as he remembered a night not so very long ago when he had thought it was all over for him; that he'd lost everything; his looks, charm, the ability to pull the birds. But that wasn't true. Liz was right. The only thing he'd ever lost was his confidence in himself.

He put a jaunty spring into his step. Juicy little bits of fluff like Dee Bastian and Josie May didn't keep hanging around him because he was Mr. Ugly Scar-face. Why, to those poor, sex-starved little village-bound creatures, he must actually seem like a glamorous film star!

CHAPTER 6

Mrs. Charles left the swami with the promise that she would call again before she returned home. With Cyril if she succeeded in persuading him to join her for the remainder of the week.

She had intended making her way slowly back to The Mermaid for lunch; but after pausing at the leaning white-painted signpost and reading the squat, waist-high warning notice beside it, she turned her back on the village and started along the narrow, slightly slippery footpath which snaked its way up and over the cliffs. It was a spur of the moment, intuitive decision. Something or someone up there on the cliffs was waiting for her to come. Now. This very minute.

Opening her handbag, she removed the picture postcard which Peggy May had enclosed with her letter. Studying the postcard, she felt she ought to be able to recognise, without too much difficulty, the small fisherman's cottage which had once been Albert and Peggy May's home. To her right, where the cliff-walks began, was a terraced row of stone and slate cottages, the last of which nestled into the craggy rock-face of the cliff and commanded quite spectacular views over the cove. Outside this cottage, set in concrete close to the footpath, was a small wooden shrine of the type commonly seen by the Austrian roadside. Sometime that morning a pilgrim had laid a bunch of pale pink roses before the wood crucifix. Mrs. Charles glanced at the shrine as she went past but did not stop.

A weather-beaten danger sign about half-way along a level stretch of ground near the top of the cliffs gave a warning to visitors not to stray too near the edge. Seated alone on a wooden bench at the side of the path and a few metres back from a buckled iron guard-rail was Tweedledee. Her hands were thrust into her coat-pockets and her ears seemed to be resting on her collar-bone, as if she had no neck. She was gazing glumly out to sea and completely ignored the clairvoyante's greeting.

Mrs. Charles paused for a moment, waiting for some response from the other woman, then gave up and moved quietly on, past a giant boulder. JUPITER'S LOOKOUT was pressed out of the thin strip of rusting metal bolted to the rock-face. The sign was heavily scored with hearts and the initials visitors to the spot had scratched into it.

Mrs. Charles looked back at the bench once. Tweedledee was still there; head morosely hunched; hands in pockets; idly swinging her legs. (Her tap-shoed feet nowhere near touched the ground.)

There was a FOR SALE board outside the tiny detached cottage which Mrs. Charles believed to be the one she sought. The place looked deserted, so she went up to the mullioned window at the front of the cottage and then, shading out the light with her hands, peered into what seemed to be a sitting-room.

A sudden noise on the rose-covered porch to her right made her drop her hands and start back guiltily. A slim, middle-aged woman wearing a scarlet nylon overall and a paisley headscarf stood in the open doorway looking at her.

"I'm sorry if I startled you," the woman said apologetically. "I don't expect Mr. Richards, the estate agent, remembered that I'd be up here this morning. The phone's been disconnected so there was no way he could contact me at the cottage and let me know that you'd be coming. You can come in and look around now, if you'd like. I've almost finished cleaning through. We won't get in one another's way."

Mrs. Charles moved away from the window. The cleaning woman had obviously mistaken her for a prospective purchaser for the property. Why give her cause to think otherwise? Smiling, the clairvoyante said, "That's very kind of you"; and stepped straight from the porch into the sitting-room.

"This is very nice," said Mrs. Charles, gazing round. The room was small and comfortable; ultra-feminine. Ugly bruise-marks left in the dark brown carpeting indicated that the room had at one time contained rather more furniture than at present.

"Yes," agreed the other woman. "It was Mrs. May's favourite. It catches the winter sun."

"You keep it beautifully," remarked Mrs. Charles, and sincerely meant it. "A home, once it's been left empty for any length of time, soon loses the personality of the people who lived in it and slowly fades and dies. But this room is vibrantly alive." She paused; looked round some more. "I gather the cottage has been empty for quite some while."

"Six months. No . . . Perhaps it's not quite as long as that. It just seems like it," the cleaning woman sighed. "A very, very long time. Mrs. May, the former owner, and I used to be close friends. That's why I offered to keep the place nice until a buyer was found for it. I know that's what my friend would've wanted, and it's the very least I can do for her. The last few weeks of her life were particularly sad, but before that, she was one of the happiest, brightest people you could've wished to know." She gazed reflectively round the room. Then, suddenly, she frowned. "I'll be glad, though, when a buyer is found. It's not healthy to do too much looking back at the past. I've been finding myself getting very depressed just lately, and I think it's because I keep coming here once a week and remembering the good days. It's time now to forget and start afresh; make new friends."

Mrs. Charles considered her thoughtfully. Then she made what she hoped would not prove to be a rash decision. "You must be the friend Peggy mentioned in her letter. Dorrie," she said.

The other woman stared at her. "You're not the clairvoyante . . . the one Peggy wrote to?" She lowered herself into a cretonne-covered armchair. "Why didn't you answer her letter?" she demanded. Her voice quavered as if she had received a nasty shock. "It would've made all the difference. Peggy would be alive today."

"I received it only last week," explained Mrs. Charles. "On Friday morning." She opened her handbag and took out the envelope which had contained Peggy May's letter. "You can see why," she said, handing it to Dorrie.

Dorrie stared bleakly at the numerous scribbled notations which had been made on the envelope by the sundry Post Offices up and down the country concerned with its delivery. "I'm sorry," she apologised brusquely. "I thought you—" She didn't bother to finish saying what she'd thought. She handed back the envelope. "At first," she went on, "Peggy didn't tell me she'd written to you. She knew what I'd say—I'm sorry," she interjected waspishly, "but I don't hold with all this fortune-telling tripe. It causes nothing but heart-break and sorrow. That's been only too plainly demonstrated to us in the past few months since there was all that publicity about Pearl Farrow. Quite a few young people in the village have got themselves hopelessly caught up in it—with very serious repercussions, I might add. One silly young girl from Sandycombe was so disturbed after a session she and her friends had with a ouija board that she took an overdose of some tablets which had been prescribed for her mother. They only just got to her in time. But that's detracting from the point," she said abruptly. "Peggy knew I wouldn't approve of what she'd done so she kept it to herself."

"What made her change her mind about telling you that she had tried to contact me?"

Dorrie frowned. "I'm not really sure. I think it was because she was so distressed and disappointed that she hadn't heard from you. As each day went by with still no word from you, she got more and more upset and depressed over what you'd told her all those years ago; she simply *had* to confide in someone. In the finish she had a nervous breakdown over it, you know. Peggy committed suicide." Dorrie's voice was bitter; condemning.

"And you hold *me* responsible for her death?"

"Yes," replied Dorrie, her tone still very bitter. Then she leaned on an elbow and covered her eyes with her hand. "No, I don't really mean that. It wasn't your fault. Peggy would never have recalled what you'd said to her if it hadn't been for Pearl Farrow. If anyone's to blame it's her." She took her hand away and looked at Mrs. Charles. "And that's nonsense too. You can't blame the poor thing for capitalising on the only piece of good luck she's ever had; a miraculous vision which saved somebody's

life. The sort of thing, I understand," she said acidly, "you clairvoyants go in for in a big way." She paused, then shook her head
and looked sad. "What a pity Peggy's letter didn't reach you in
time."

"In time for what?"

"To stop Peggy taking her life."

"Do you honestly believe that the prompt delivery of her letter
to me would've made any difference?"

Dorrie looked puzzled. "But—" She didn't finish.

"I don't have the power of life and death, you know," said the
clairvoyante quietly.

"That's a very callous thing to say."

"Perhaps, but it's the truth. If I chose to end my life, and sincerely meant to carry out that wish, there's absolutely nothing
that anyone could do to prevent my doing so."

Dorrie was staring at her angrily. "If you're trying to tell me
that this was what Peggy really wanted, then I'm sorry, as a clairvoyante you're about as gifted as Pearl Farrow is; and that isn't
saying much for either one of you!" Her voice cracked with emo-
tion. "Peggy loved life—every minute of it."

"Not at the end she didn't," said Mrs. Charles imperturbably.
"Her life became a nightmare; a living hell."

Dorrie's face contorted in an ugly grimace. "And I suppose
the cards told you that," she sneered. "Or was it the ouija
board?" she asked sarcastically.

Mrs. Charles did not answer. There was a hostile silence between the two women. Then, at length, the clairvoyante said,
"It's true, isn't it?"

Dorrie stared at her for a moment, then covered her face with
her hands and burst into tears.

Mrs. Charles crossed slowly to the window and stood looking
out over the cove. The sky had turned an ever duller grey; it
looked like rain. After a moment, she turned her attention to the
cliffs and Jupiter's Lookout. Tweedledee had left the bench and
was now wandering aimlessly towards the cottage, moodily
scuffing the path with the toes of her shoes and with her hands
still thrust deep into her coat-pockets. Her unexpected reap-

pearance made the clairvoyante feel uneasy. She continued to watch the strange little woman until Dorrie, recovering herself, said reproachfully, "Why did you come here?"

"Do you really want to know the answer to that question," the clairvoyante asked, turning, "or is this merely your way of saying you wish I'd kept away and left you to enjoy wallowing in your misery and grief over your friend's passing?"

Dorrie looked at her dully. "You're a very hard woman."

"I am when I want to get at the truth. And I think you know what the truth is."

"The truth?" Dorrie rubbed the back of her hand slowly across her damp cheeks. "The truth about what?"

"Peggy— The traumatic event in her life which brought about her dramatic change of personality. I think that somewhere deep down in your subconscious you know, or suspect you know, why she went from a happy-go-lucky, fun-loving person to a nervous wreck. And that, I also think, is what is really troubling you and causing your depression."

"That's absolute nonsense. I haven't the least idea—" Dorrie broke off; stared vaguely into space. Then, after a very long moment: "Peggy and her husband were very close. He died, you know, about three months before she wrote to you." Her voice tailed off. For the moment she seemed to be lost in thought and considering something which Mrs. Charles suspected had not occurred to her before. The clairvoyante allowed her time to think things over before asking:

"How long were you and Peggy friends?"

"All our lives. We grew up together . . . went to the same schools—did everything together. We were only apart during the time she went off to become a dancer."

"Then you know why she died," said Mrs. Charles quietly.

"No," said Dorrie firmly, shaking her head quickly.

Mrs. Charles smiled at her. "Your whole attitude over your friend's death screams that truth at me. The answer is there and you know it's there, but you've turned away from it because it's beyond your comprehension. Your spirit—your inner self—is seriously disturbed and will continue to be disturbed until you let go of the truth which is struggling to be free."

Dorrie looked at her; frowned. "That's the sort of thing those spiritualists who were down here from London last week-end said about Pearl Farrow. They said she was a disturbed adolescent; that's why the spirits picked on her. They said the spirits deliberately pick out someone like her to do their work for them." A strange expression crossed her face. "Pearl stands to make a fortune, I've heard it said; you know, from personal appearances on television and interviews in women's magazines—the story of her life . . . all that tripe! That's if Mary, the girl's mother, can be persuaded to let Pearl be interviewed."

Mrs. Charles considered her thoughtfully. "I'm trying to make up my mind," she confessed after a small pause, "whether it's Pearl Farrow you don't like, or her clairvoyance."

Dorrie gave a start. "Pearl? Nonsense," she said briskly. "She's only a child. God forbid that I should ever bear malice towards a child. And that's all Pearl is, a seventeen-year-old child who has never grown up and never will. The poor girl has the mentality of a nine-year-old. It's her mother I don't like," she snapped.

"Why not?" the clairvoyante asked quietly.

Dorrie gave another start. She looked genuinely shocked. A puzzled frown furrowed her brow. "I don't know. That just came out. Now what on earth would make me say a stupid thing like that?" she wondered out loud. She widened her eyes at the clairvoyante. "I don't even know the woman all that well. They keep themselves very much to themselves. Always have done." She gazed absently past the clairvoyante at the window. "Perhaps that's what made me say what I did. Yes—" she nodded slowly "—that's probably it; a subconscious dislike of somebody who has never wanted to be friendly with any of us." She spoke vaguely, as if to herself. Then, after a slight hesitation, she looked directly at Mrs. Charles and said, "You know, it's a funny thing, but for weeks now I've had this peculiar tight feeling inside me as if I've been holding something in, something I was afraid to say. And now I feel ever so much better. Almost relieved."

"Then we are making some progress; we're loosening the chains which are holding your true, inner self in bondage. Let's see if we can't get rid of them altogether."

"But *how?*" Dorrie frowned earnestly at the clairvoyante. "I've already told you that I don't really know why I dislike Mary Farrow. I'm only guessing when I say it's probably because she doesn't really want to have anything to do with us, everybody else in the village. The only thing I know for certain is that I feel better for having let the truth about my feelings in that quarter out into the open."

"It's only part of the truth; the key to the door. Now we must use that key to turn the lock on the door to the whole picture."

"Why?" asked Dorrie curiously. "What is it to you why Peggy took her life and how I feel about it?"

"Let's just say I care and leave it at that for the moment," replied the clairvoyante.

Dorrie gazed at her for a long time without saying anything. Then she nodded slowly and said, "You know, I believe you really do care. But I don't think it's about us, Peggy and me—" She broke off with a nervous laugh. "There, you've got me talking like you, a clairvoyante. The next thing you know I'll be gazing in a crystal ball!" She smiled tremulously and the first glimmer of friendship showed in her eyes. "Very well then," she said. "I've given you the key, now use it and we'll see where it leads us. Please sit down and make yourself comfortable." She looked embarrassed, also apprehensive as she rose and indicated to the sofa. "This could take some time . . ."

CHAPTER 7

"Well," said Mrs. Charles when she was comfortably settled on the sofa and Dorrie had resumed her seat. "So far we've managed to establish that you don't like Mrs. Farrow and that you've no conscious knowledge of the real reason for your animosity towards her; also, that you bear Pearl Farrow no ill will. What about Mr. Farrow?"

"He's dead," said Dorrie. "He was killed in a freak accident on the farm where he was employed as a labourer. I never knew him: I don't think anyone else in the village did either. Mary Farrow left Michaelmas Cove as a young girl—like Peggy did; only in Mary's case she went into domestic service on a big estate outside Sandycombe."

Mrs. Charles held up a hand. "Forgive me for interrupting . . . Peggy *came* from here? This was where she was born?"

Dorrie seemed bewildered. "Yes. I was born here too. So, for that matter, was Mary Farrow. I told you . . . Peggy and I grew up together. Why do you ask?"

Mrs. Charles said hesitatingly, "I obviously misunderstood Peggy. I gathered the impression from her letter that she came here to Michaelmas Cove for the first time as a young bride."

The other woman was shaking her head. "Albert May and Peggy were childhood sweethearts. There was the devil to pay when she left home to take up dancing. It had always been understood between them that one day they'd marry. Then Peggy got this bee in her bonnet about wanting to be a dancer and seeing a bit of life before settling down. I personally have always felt that to begin with, it was all talk—romanticising—and that she'd never have done anything about a dancing career if Albert hadn't got so high-handed with her about it. They had the most awful row. Instead of waiting for her to grow out of the phase she was going through, Albert told her she had to choose—him or her dancing (she was a beautiful natural dancer); and Peggy simply up and left. She was dreadfully upset about it, but Albert pushed her into it. I was with her while she was packing her things. She cried the whole time and I remember her saying that if she gave in to Albert, let him see that he could get his own way and dictate to her how she should live her life, they'd never be happy together.

"Anyway," sighed Dorrie, "off she went. She wrote to me regularly . . . I've still got most of her letters. For a long time she was quite miserable and homesick, then she seemed to cheer up a bit. She didn't say as much, but I suspected that there was some new man in her life." She smiled quickly. "That would've been typical of Peggy. Then—I forget now exactly how long it was after she left, but it must've been something like two to three years later—Albert went after her. There was a reconciliation and he brought her back home.

"But to get back to Mary Farrow. She left here (I don't suppose she would've been much more than sixteen or seventeen at the time) and went to work for Sir Percival Easterbrook as a parlourmaid. As I've said, I've never really been closely acquainted with her. She's four or five years older than I am. Her parents were well on in years when she came along and were a bit strange (like she is)—very Victorian in their attitudes, but without all the hypocrisy—and they'd never let her mix with us, Peggy and me. Or with any of the other young people in the village. Her mother used to bring her to school every day, then be waiting outside the gate in the afternoon to fetch her home again—" Dorrie's eyebrows shot straight up "—and that went on right up until the time she left home to go to work on the Easterbrook estate. Mary used to come home occasionally to see the old people; first the two of them, and then just her father after her mother died. Then old Mr. O'Connell—Mary's father—had a massive stroke. Very suddenly, as I recall it," she said pensively. "I overheard my father discussing it with my mother—my father was the village doctor. The night Mary came round to fetch him over to see to Mr. O'Connell was about the most I've ever heard Mary say, then and since! I answered the door and she asked if the doctor was in and would he come right away as '*her pa,*' Mary said—" Dorrie smiled self-consciously "—'*had been took real queer.*' Then she said would someone please telephone or send for the father to come quickly."

"The father? A priest, you mean?"

Dorrie nodded. "After Mr. O'Connell went—he died that same night—we didn't see Mary again for a very long time; and in the meanwhile, she'd married Jim Farrow and had Pearl. Pearl was about five or six when she and her mother came back here to live. Mr. O'Connell had left Mary some money and there was still the old home. And with Pearl the way she is, I don't suppose Mary could think of going back into domestic service . . . after her husband's death, I mean. Pearl's not violent, but her mother has always needed to keep a fairly close watch on her; mainly, I think, to protect Pearl from herself."

"Would you say that Mrs. Farrow inherited a lot of money from her father's estate?"

"I don't really know. Quite frankly, I've never given it any thought."

"How had he earned a living?"

"He was a cobbler. A very good one too. Lady Easterbrook had a badly deformed foot and Mr. O'Connell made her shoes; in all the latest fashions. She wouldn't have anyone else make footwear for her. That was probably how Mary got work on the Easterbrook estate."

"Isn't it a little unlikely that Mrs. Farrow's father would've made enough money as a village cobbler to leave her and her mentally retarded child comfortably off for all these years?"

"I wouldn't exactly say they are *comfortably* off. They've managed—by the looks of things, with a bit of a struggle. And over the years, Mary's taken in the odd paying guest or two. But only during the holiday season. It's fairly common practice: most of us make ends meet by doing a little of that sort of thing in summer. Mary could probably even do a whole lot better than she does if only she'd stop being so fussy about who she takes in."

Dorrie paused and made a face. "Mary's a bit funny about men—if you know what I mean." Her eyebrows rose meaningfully. "She'll walk right past the local tradesmen's shops if they're serving behind the counter and not their wives or a female assistant. It's quite a joke in the village. Everyone was absolutely amazed when word got around that she'd married *and* had a child. We simply couldn't imagine 'Mary, Mary Quite Contrary' (that's what we all used to call her when we were children!) getting wed. She'd go all red-faced and tongue-tied, or turn tail and flee if she happened to see any of the village boys walking towards her when she was out alone. Which wasn't often. We used to tease her unmercifully . . . *Mary, Mary Quite Contrary, ooh, look how your knickers grow!*"

A smile flashed across Dorrie's face. "Mary's mother used to make her wear dreadfully old-fashioned bloomers—'neck to knees,' my mother called them; and poor Mary hated them so much that she'd stitch lengths of elastic to the hems of her skirts and then hook the loops of elastic under the heels of her shoes so that her skirts wouldn't ride up and reveal her bloomers while she was pedalling her bicycle around the village. 'Chastity belts,' the boys called them—the pieces of elastic, that is," she remembered with a grin. "They were very cruel to her."

She hesitated. Then, continuing:

"You never know, but that could be why I don't like her. Because she took everything we handed out to her without a murmur and always turned the other cheek or ran and hid behind her mother's skirts. And maybe," she went on with a dry laugh, "that's why Mary has never had any time for us. She's probably never forgiven us for the way we treated her when we were children."

Dorrie considered the possibility for a moment or two, then shrugged it off. She looked at the clairvoyante expectantly and Mrs. Charles nodded and said:

"Can you tell me about the weeks between Peggy's sitting down and writing to me and her death? I appreciate that Peggy wouldn't have been her normal self during those weeks, but what form did her anxiety take? Was she depressed? Overexcitable, perhaps?"

Dorrie frowned reflectively. "Neither, though not everyone would agree with me there. That comment I made earlier about Peggy's relationship with her husband . . . Everybody said that she was depressed and grief-stricken over Albert's death, but *nobody*—" she said with an emphatic shake of her head "—knew her as well as I did. She was upset and, I believe, grieved very deeply and sincerely over Albert's passing, but not abnormally so. In those weeks after he went, she retreated into herself. She had something on her mind. Something was worrying her."

"Can you give me some idea of time? Peggy wrote to me on the fourteenth of June . . . How long was that after her husband's death; and how long after that again was it that she herself died?"

"Let me see . . ." Dorrie paused and cast her mind back. "Albert died in March; on the seventeenth, I think it was. No, that was the day of the funeral; St. Patrick's Day. Fr. Thomas—who was rather partial to his pint of ale—had been, to put it kindly, somewhat thirstier than usual. (Albert was a Catholic: Peggy wasn't.) The funeral had to be delayed for a time while Fr. Thomas pulled himself together. Anyway, Albert died sometime during the preceding week." She hesitated and a peculiar, in a way almost embarrassed, expression crossed her face. "The fourteenth," she said abruptly. "Albert died on the fourteenth of March. Peggy was deeply distressed and upset, naturally; but as I've said," she went on, a note of caution creeping into her voice, "there was something else as well, a preoccupation with her thoughts. Which was most unusual for her." A small, self-conscious smile flickered momentarily on Dorrie's lips. "Peggy was inclined to be something of a butterfly-brain: it wasn't her nature to worry too much about anything."

"Did she have any financial problems?"

Dorrie smiled. "Don't let appearances fool you." She glanced round the modestly furnished room. "All the good stuff has gone. Both Albert and Peggy were very close with money, Peggy more so than Albert; but that isn't to say there wasn't much of it around. There were stories—" She paused and shrugged. "You know, about Albert and that boat of his. Some of the trips he made—well, they weren't all fishing trips. Albert's family—the Mays—have nearly all gone now, either died or drifted away from Michaelmas Cove looking for work, so I'm not really hurting anybody when I say they've always had a reputation for being a little bit casual about some of the jobs they'd take on." She paused again. Then, shaking her head: "No, I'd be very surprised if it were that—money troubles. And anyway, I don't think Peggy was worried so much as she had something on her mind and was wrestling with her conscience about it."

Mrs. Charles looked at her speculatively. "You had some reason for thinking that her conscience might've been troubling her?"

Dorrie spread out her hands on her lap and studied them. "This is a very small place," she said at length. "No matter how careful and circumspect you are, you can be sure someone will see what you're up to and catch you out. Peggy never mentioned anything to me about it until I raised the matter with her." She looked up at Mrs. Charles with a quick frown. "And I wouldn't want you to think I was prying. I was genuinely concerned about what people would think. The man had asked about her in the village (this was some while before Albert passed on—the best part of a year, I'd say), and there'd been whispered talk then, especially as he'd inquired after her by her maiden name, Baldwin. That was bad enough. Then I bumped into him—the same man— on the cliffs the night Albert died. I was coming away from here after seeing Peggy and it was fairly obvious to me that this was where he was heading. I was naturally curious to know who he was and what he'd wanted. I pretended that I thought he was somebody from Albert's lodge who was calling to see him before he passed on and to ask Peggy if there were any help she needed. I didn't let on that I knew he was *her* friend, someone who had known her when she was Peggy Baldwin—"

CHAPTER 8

A sudden, sharp metallic sound made both women start. Their eyes flew to the door, the source of the sound; and then, after a hesitant pause, Dorrie said, "It's nothing. The metal flap on the mail-slot sometimes gets stuck fast after children have been playing about on the porch and interfering with it, and then later on it suddenly frees itself and snaps back into position."

Mrs. Charles looked unconvinced. Rising, she crossed to the window and gazed out across the cliffs. There was no one about. Not even Tweedledee.

The clairvoyante returned to the sofa. "I thought I heard something else," she said, sitting down again. "Someone on the porch."

Dorrie gave her a searching look but made no comment. "Where was I?" she asked. "Oh, yes; this man . . . Peggy got quite annoyed with me about him and told me I was becoming a proper old village busybody. And when I pointed out to her that the way *she* was carrying on, anyone would think he was an old flame—" Dorrie made a low whistling sound "—she really hit the roof and said he was nothing of the sort; just someone she'd known a very long while ago—a good friend and nothing more."

"But you didn't believe her."

Dorrie's eyes widened. "The way she was going on about him?" She smiled and shook her head. "Of course not. And yet—" She paused and scratched her cheek thoughtfully. "I know this sounds terribly unkind, but he was so, well, not really ugly but, you know—" she shrugged "—not Peggy's type at all. He had a nasty scar—a burn, I think—down one side of his face, and Peggy only ever had an eye for a good-looking man (I'm talking now about when she was footloose and fancy-free; single). Albert was an uncommonly handsome man. All the girls in the village, including me—" she smiled "—positively swooned over him." She paused; frowned thoughtfully. "It was her whole attitude over this stranger and my mentioning him to her: she had to be guilty about something. Besides . . ."

Dorrie hesitated; picked at a loose thread sprouting from one of the buttons on her overall.

"Yes?" the clairvoyante prompted her when she said no more and the silence lengthened.

"Well, there was another reason for my thinking that she had a boy-friend on the side. As far as I know she was always faithful to Albert, but she was a *very* attractive woman; the pretty, fluffy type. Men liked her and she liked them." Dorrie looked up and smiled self-consciously. "I've always blamed my friendship with her for my never having married. All the young men I brought home took one look at my friend Peggy and that was it. Back on the shelf went Doris Kemp!" she said without any bitterness.

"You think Peggy had been meeting someone—the man with the disfigured face—secretly."

"Yes." Dorrie nodded. "I saw her myself time and time again going down the cliff-face to the old caves." Dorrie looked troubled. "You've got to understand that Albert was bedridden for quite a long time before he died—almost a year. I wasn't criticising Peggy; I simply felt that as I'd seen her going down to the caves regularly once a month somebody else was bound to have seen her too, even though the path down the cliff-face is fairly well concealed from Jupiter's Lookout. I know the caves are supposed to be inaccessible by land, but I can remember my father telling me that there's a way in. 'If you know where to look,' he said, 'and your surname happens to be May.' Anyway—" she sighed "—I was sure people would start gossiping."

"So you went one step further and told her what you suspected?"

"Yes." Dorrie nodded again. "I asked her outright if this man was the reason why she went down to the caves once a month."

"And what did she say?"

" '*Watch the wall, m'darlin' while t'gentlemen goes by.*' "

The clairvoyante's eyes widened. "Mind your own business and look the other way?"

Dorrie gave her a wry look. "Hereabouts that particular piece of advice has a special significance. I don't know how true it is—it was a bit before my time," she put in with a quick smile, "but that's supposed to be what the villagers did way back in the eighteenth century when Michaelmas Cove was a smugglers' haven. On the nights when the smugglers were meeting the boat from France, the villagers—those who weren't themselves actively engaged in the smuggling—locked and bolted their doors and drew all the curtains; made quite sure they didn't see anything of what was going on. And there must be some truth in the story: the monks who operated the smuggling ring would never have managed to hoodwink the King's men for as long as they did if they hadn't had the full co-operation of everyone in the village. The contraband kegs of brandy were rowed ashore and then off-loaded into the caves by the men of the village under the supervision of the prior from the priory outside Sandycombe and kept hidden there until the monks arrived with donkeys to collect them. Or so the story goes."

Mrs. Charles was nodding thoughtfully. "So in other words, Peggy wanted you to believe that this was what she was doing . . . Going down to the caves once a month to pick up some kind of modern-day contraband?"

Dorrie shrugged. "It wasn't impossible. She'd started going down there about a month after Albert took to his bed; and there have always been rumours in the village that Albert was actively engaged in the village forefathers' pursuits and smuggling in brandy from France on his fishing boat. Others in the village too." She smiled. "It's only the law of the land that says it's wrong to smuggle liquor. Here it's a tradition, both the smuggling *and* the violation of the law. None of the brandy I saw drunk in my father's house ever came from any legally licenced premises! My guess is that there's still probably some of it going on, if only for tradition's sake."

"Was it on a certain, specific day of each month that Peggy would go down the cliffs to the caves?"

Dorrie nodded. "On the fourteenth of every month. Around eight in the evening. At least that was when I spotted her slipping away down there."

"Did you ever see anyone else on any of these occasions?"

Dorrie shook her head. "Whoever she was meeting—the man I mentioned or someone else—must've got there well ahead of her." She hesitated and the red blotches on her throat which Mrs. Charles had noticed several minutes earlier grew steadily larger and darker.

The clairvoyante remained silent and waited patiently until Dorrie felt able to give vent to the cause of her obvious inner distress.

"It sounds awful now," Dorrie continued when the growing silence became the more uncomfortable of the two to bear. "And I hate having to admit it. I waited once to see who was with her when she left the caves to go home; but," she said, wide-eyed, "she was alone."

Mrs. Charles looked at her contemplatively. "If Peggy were involved in smuggling on her husband's behalf—receiving illicit goods (say, brandy from France, like in the old days)—then surely she would've needed quite a lot of help, more than that of just one man, to bring the kegs up the cliffs from the caves and then down again into the village?"

"Somebody could've come round the coast by boat. That's what the monks used to do when they were passed the word that the King's men were lying in wait for them in the village. If Peggy had taken over from Albert—and I'm not saying that he was a smuggler, you understand!—then that's probably what did happen. Someone—whoever she went down there to meet—brought a boat into the cove and took the contraband out the same way. But I still say she was meeting an old flame, if not the man I ran into on the cliffs, then someone else, someone whom I believe she met while she was single and away dancing. And then when Albert became ill, Peggy and this man renewed their friendship, meeting clandestinely once a month in the caves. However, as time dragged on, Peggy's man-friend—and for argument's sake, we'll say it was the same one I bumped into on the night Albert died—got impatient, and instead of sticking to the usual plan and meeting Peggy in the caves (I think he must've known that Albert was sinking fast), he threw caution to the wind and came here to the cottage to see her. I don't know . . . What I *do* know is that Peggy was badly upset by his visit—I felt because of his lack of respect for a dying man—and I'm convinced that it aroused in her deep feelings of guilt over their relationship. I never saw her go down to the caves again. On the fourteenth, or at any other time of the month."

"Isn't it just possible that her failure to go down there any more meant that her smuggling activities on her husband's behalf ceased on his death?"

Dorrie shrugged non-committally, but the hard set of her mouth and the sceptical look in her eye suggested that if she were forced to choose, she would prefer her notions of a secret lover from the past to the smuggling theory.

Mrs. Charles turned to something else. "When did Peggy start to worry about the hermit and Pearl Farrow in relation to the warning I'd given her?"

The question took Dorrie by surprise. Her eyes grew wide. "What's all this about a hermit? Peggy never mentioned anything like that to me."

"It was one of the things worrying her. She said so very clearly in her letter."

Dorrie shook her head. "There's the hermit of the local legend," she said slowly. "The ghost of the old prior; the smuggler."

"Yes, she mentioned the legend. However, I feel we are looking for someone with a great deal more substance to him than mere ghost form."

"Well, there's Fr. Thomas, I suppose," Dorrie said doubtfully. "I daresay you could call him a hermit of sorts. But that's ridiculous; really stretching the imagination to link him with what was troubling her. They were the very best of friends. As a child, Fr. Thomas lived for a time with Albert's family as one of their own. He was an orphan. The Church placed him with the Mays and he stayed with them until he entered the monastery. He and Albert were as close as brothers."

"I understand that Fr. Thomas wears a habit of the type one usually associates with a religious hermit."

"Yes, sometimes. But in recent years I have just as often seen him dressed in ordinary everyday wear. Without the brown habit or a dog-collar, I mean. But only when he's relaxing and off duty, of course."

"This is permissible?"

"With Fr. Thomas' particular order? Yes, apparently so. I'm not a Catholic, so I don't really know all that much about it, but I rather fancy that this freedom of dress is something which has been introduced over the last few years as a result of the more liberal attitude the Church now appears to be adopting towards this kind of thing."

"You're quite sure Peggy never expressed a dislike of him? Fear, perhaps?"

"Never," said Dorrie with an emphatic shake of her head. "He's a great character and everybody in the village was extremely sorry to see him go. He had to retire for health reasons. Not so very long after Albert went." She widened her eyes expressively and slowly shook her head. "I simply cannot believe that Peggy had anything at all to fear from Michael Thomas. That poor man has only ever been one person's enemy. His own. The demon drink," she explained and grimaced. "He and Albert always drank more than was good for them; though to give Albert his due, he did moderate his drinking to some extent after his first heart attack a few years back. But before that one was as bad as the other."

Mrs. Charles nodded thoughtfully, then moved on to Pearl Farrow but again drew a blank. Dorrie could think of no reason why her friend should have feared the girl and her alleged powers of clairvoyance. In her opinion, this was about as likely to have been what was really troubling Peggy as the suggestion that she was afraid of Fr. Thomas; and made even less sense.

The clairvoyante left the cottage ten minutes later, satisfied up to a point with what she had learned but troubled by the fact that the real truth about Peggy May and the events of the few months preceding her death was as safely locked away in Doris Kemp's subconscious as it had ever been. There she had failed. Completely.

CHAPTER 9

Dorrie collected up her things. Then, closing the front door of the cottage behind her, she started off across the cliffs.

It was a few minutes after two. The sun had long since disappeared behind the heavy black clouds which were spreading with menacing rapidity over the distant horizon and moving stealthily towards Michaelmas Cove. A chill wind had sprung up and she felt cold after her morning's activity within the cosy confines of the small cottage. She was anxious to get home before it rained and yet each step that she took grew slower and slower in tune with her thoughts. At Jupiter's Lookout she paused and gazed out over the steadily rising sea. A low, slow-moving cloud enveloped her in a fine, damp mist.

"Why don't I like Mary Farrow?" she asked herself for what must have been the twentieth time since Mrs. Charles had said good-bye and left her to finish her chores. "Why? What has Mary Farrow ever done to you, Doris Kemp?"

Frowning, she lowered herself onto the bench near the guard-rail. Then suddenly, in a split second, she was transported back over a quarter of a century to her late parents' home. She could hear her father's deep voice coming from the sitting-room. He was talking to someone. She had heard him come in a few minutes earlier after having gone with Mary O'Connell to attend on her father. Dorrie had a message for him— *The Forresters' baby had come down with the croup; it was urgent; would the doctor come right away* . . .

In her mind's eye, Dorrie watched the young teenaged girl she had once been putting her hand on the sitting-room doorknob. Her father's voice had dropped abruptly to a tone he used only when he was very disturbed about something.

"Mary killed him, Mother."

A sickening feeling swept over Dorrie as it all came back to her.

She remembered the pause, *the dreadful pause*, before her mother responded.

"What are you going to do about it, Edgar?" her mother had finally asked in that calm, matter-of-fact voice that Dorrie remembered so well.

"Nothing," Dorrie heard her father's voice say in reply. *"Mary will have to—"*

Dorrie the teenager was suddenly in the room staring at her parents.

The look on her face must have given her away for her father had turned on her angrily and said:

"Whatever it was that you just heard, my girl, you put it right out of your head forever. And let that be a lesson to you. No good ever came of listening at keyholes!"

"I wasn't, Papa," Dorrie could hear herself protesting. *"I didn't hear anything; I swear it!"*

Dorrie's spine stiffened with shock. She sat bolt upright on the bench and gazed intently into space. "But I *did* hear something," she said in an awed whisper. "I heard my father tell my mother that Mary O'Connell had killed her father."

"But how?" she asked herself. Mr. O'Connell had been an absolute giant of a man; strong as an ox. Dorrie laughed nervously. Perhaps something came over Mary once she left home to go and work on the Easterbrook estate and the change in her shocked her father to death!

The gritty scrunching sound of gravel underfoot made her start. Anxiously, she twisted round on the bench. The mist had grown heavier without her realising it. All that she could see distinctly was a pair of black-shoed feet. Someone was standing there watching her. (A woman? She wasn't sure.)

A dark, shapeless blur loomed over her: then, slowly, as she rose, her searching gaze brought the blur into focus and every inch of it became sharply defined . . .

Heavy black woollen topcoat buttoned almost to the throat, its collar turned up against the cold, grey felt hat worn well down on the head; and, finally, the face beneath the hat.

A pang of fear went through her. "What d'you think you're doing?" she demanded, a note of panic sharpening her voice. "What do you want?" She moved around the bench; backed away from the guard-rail and the cliff-edge. "Why are you staring at me like that?"

There was one of those awesome silences, that impression of time and space standing perfectly still which immediately precedes extreme personal danger. And then that moment was upon her.

And it was all so unreal.

The last thought that Doris Kemp ever had.

The clairvoyante went out again at three that afternoon and made her way back to the Old Quarter. The heavy sea mist which had swallowed up Michaelmas Cove soon after two o'clock had lifted as quickly as it had descended, but it was still overcast and dull. It had rained heavily a short while earlier, leaving the roads awash, the lanes deserted.

Mrs. Charles bought a bar of chocolate at the grocer's shop in Lamppost Lane, but only because she was out of small change and would need some that night for the pay phone in the hall at The Mermaid. Then she walked around the corner into French-man's Lane. She stopped outside the oak-panelled door of the terrace cottage next door to the shop and knocked softly. While she waited, she glanced up and down the lane, then at the sky. The cold air was damp on her face; heavy with moisture. More rain clouds were gathering.

Keeping an eye on the clouds, she knocked again, a little more loudly and insistently. The net on the window to the left of the door was suddenly twitched aside and Ida Claythorpe's grey head bobbed into view. A look of recognition crossed the old lady's face and she gestured to her caller, by means of a series of hand signs, that the door was open and she wished her to enter.

Mrs. Charles nodded and pushed gently on the door which gave way under her hand.

"I'm in here," Mrs. Claythorpe called out from her sitting-room as Mrs. Charles paused in the narrow hall to close the door behind her. "Chair-bound," Mrs. Claythorpe added.

The clairvoyante entered the tiny front room and smiled at Mrs. Claythorpe who was sitting propped up with pillows in a straight-backed armchair. Her heavily bandaged right leg was supported on a brown leather ottoman. There was a coal fire burning brightly in the grate and the room was cosy and warm.

"Sorry about that," said Mrs. Claythorpe, motioning to Mrs. Charles to take off her suede jacket. "I heard you knock the first time but I thought it was my ministering angel from the shop next door with my tea. That's why the door was on the latch."

"I'm sorry if I've disturbed you," said Mrs. Charles, removing her jacket and headscarf and laying them neatly over the back of a chair, "but I was out walking and I thought I'd call in to see what progress you're making. Penny told me about your accident."

"Take a pew." Mrs. Claythorpe waved her visitor into a chair near the hearth. "Don't stand on ceremony; it makes me tired just looking at you!" The old lady squirmed a little in her seat in an attempt to make herself more comfortable and winced as the movement jarred her injured leg and ankle.

"I see you're still in some pain," observed Mrs. Charles.

"Oh, it's not too bad. What peeves and pains me is that now everybody can say, *'We told you so!'*" Mrs. Claythorpe smiled ruefully. "The way everyone goes on, everybody would think they've got stolen treasure buried up there that they're afraid I'm going to stumble across." She gave Mrs. Charles a knowing look. "They don't really like it, you know; outsiders like me tramping all over their precious cliffs. A throw-back to the old smuggling days; a genetic nervousness that's been handed down from one generation to the next."

"How long have you lived here?"

"Ten years, give or take a few months. I came down on holiday one year and liked it so much I decided to stay."

"Surely after having lived here for all this time no one would consider you to be an outsider?"

"Don't you believe it, m'dear. I could live here for another ten years, and another ten years on top of that, and still be on the outer where their precious cliffs are concerned. I do it to aggravate 'em, you know." Mrs. Claythorpe laughed; a deep, rich throaty sound. "One of the few pleasures I get out of life nowadays. Plenty of other places I could go for a walk. Damn sight safer for me too, at my age." She smiled broadly. "Ah well, no doubt I'll come to real grief up there one of these days and then they'll really have the last laugh."

"It seems to be quite the fashionable thing to do, even with people who have lived here all their lives and know how dangerous the cliffs are."

"Oho!" said Mrs. Claythorpe, eyeing the clairvoyante thoughtfully. "Who's been talking to you? Not one of the locals, I'll bet."

Mrs. Charles smiled. "Is it really all that unlikely that one of the villagers would illustrate the dangers of cliff-walking by telling me of the accidents which have befallen people up there recently?"

"That's the very last thing they'd do," Mrs. Claythorpe assured her. "You're dealing with a rare bird here! Most definitely you'd be given a strongly worded warning about the dangers of walking on the cliffs, but a warning and no more. Then, if you chose to disregard their wise advice, they'd simply draw up a chair and sit down and watch and wait for the inevitable to happen. Great believers in the broadening of one's knowledge by personal experience. Stoics, the lot of 'em! And anyway, what accidents? There haven't been any serious accidents up there for donkey's years. A suicide but no accidents."

"Didn't the local priest, Fr. Thomas, slip and fall accidentally some months back?"

The old lady snorted. "Fr. Thomas either jumped or he was pushed; and he wouldn't jump, suicide being the mortal sin that it is, so he was pushed. That man is as agile as a mountain goat, even in his skirts and with a tankful of ale in him. Oh no—" She pursed her lips and shook her head. "Michael Thomas didn't do any falling. I've seen him with my own two eyes, nipping over the cliffs in that long brown habit of his as if he'd got wings on his feet. Mind you, I'm the only one who thinks so." Her head moved slowly up and down and there was an omniscient look in her eye. "But this is one time where I've got it all over them, the locals. Michael Thomas and I would often run into one another up there as he was on his way to visit the fishermen's cottages. I know exactly how sure of foot that man really is. Good Lord, he's been going up there for years; all his life. He could do it blindfold in a howling blizzard and never put a foot wrong."

"Who would want to push him over a cliff?"

"A good question. Who indeed? I personally haven't the faintest idea."

"Wouldn't Fr. Thomas know if someone pushed him over the cliff-edge?"

"He says he wasn't pushed."

"Does that mean someone else thinks like you; that it wasn't an accident?"

"No." Mrs. Claythorpe smiled enigmatically. "I asked Michael Thomas outright to his face; told him to swear before Almighty God that he wasn't pushed that night."

"And?"

The old lady's eyes twinkled at Mrs. Charles. "He lectured me on the taking of the Lord's Name in vain. Which, as far as I was concerned, answered my question. Michael Thomas was pushed all right. And he knows that I know it! Drops in on me every so often . . . I'm not a Catholic, but—" She hesitated; then, with a quick smile: "He says he's concerned about my spiritual well-being. A lot of double-talk really. It's his way of advising me to keep my suspicions to myself. That's if I want to continue to live a long and healthy life."

"That sounds more like a threat to me."

"Perhaps, but then you don't know him, do you? He's a good man, and I honestly think he's frightened for me—why, I don't know. I've never made any secret of the fact that I believe what I believe. Nothing has happened to me yet. Though if one were to take note of what some people say, then my number is well and truly up anyway and I'm dicing with death every time I step outside my front door." Mrs. Claythorpe grinned cheerfully. "Silly arses!"

"Including Pearl Farrow?"

"Ah, so you've heard about her too." Mrs. Claythorpe was silent for a moment. She looked at Mrs. Charles, then pointed to the fire, which was dying down, and Mrs. Charles obediently rose and stoked it and added some more fuel.

"You're different," said Mrs. Claythorpe when Mrs. Charles was done. "I spotted that the moment I first saw you back there at The Mermaid. You're not the regular tourist type we see. You're down here on some kind of errand, aren't you?" She cocked her head to one side and narrowed her eyes. "No, don't tell me. Let me guess. You're one of these investigative journalists. Am I right?"

Mrs. Charles solemnly shook her head.

Mrs. Claythorpe pulled thoughtfully on her chin. "You know about the hermit, Michaelmas Cove's ghost: you call on old Ranji (I saw you this morning!); and now you're here quizzing me. And you are quizzing me, m'dear. Ida Claythorpe knows when she's being quizzed! Now why would you be interested in ghosts and accidents on cliffs and Pearl Farrow, our local prophetess?"

"I'm a clairvoyante," said Mrs. Charles.

"Saints preserve us!" Mrs. Claythorpe threw up her hands in the air and then slapped them down on her thighs. "Not another one running amok with a ouija board!"

Mrs. Charles smiled. "I heard about that. Was Pearl Farrow in any way involved? Wouldn't she and the girl concerned—the one who took the overdose—be of an age?"

Mrs. Claythorpe's expression was inscrutable and gave no hint of what was actually passing through her mind. After a small pause, she said, "Pearl's probably a little bit younger—by about a couple of years, I'd say. But I doubt that the girl who tried to commit suicide—a lass from Sandycombe—would know her. Personally, I mean. The Farrows keep themselves very much to themselves. You know about Pearl, I suppose; that she's mentally retarded?"

Mrs. Charles nodded.

"I've seen Pearl Farrow no more than a dozen times in all the years that I've lived here. Understandable . . . Not that I approve of that sort of behaviour myself," said Mrs. Claythorpe quickly. "And one can't help wondering why some parents act this way. Are they really thinking of their poor unfortunate offspring, or are they simply ashamed and embarrassed for themselves?"

"Pearl Farrow is as obviously subnormal as all that?"

"Oh yes," said Mrs. Claythorpe with feeling. "Mind you, not everyone would be able to see it as clearly as I can. I had a younger brother like it. Never aged mentally beyond eight or nine. He died in his thirties, but he looked little more than a child. That was what I meant when I said I didn't approve of Mrs. Farrow's attitude over Pearl. My mother was a very sensible, loving woman. We never pretended about my brother and were never ashamed or embarrassed by his affliction. We all loved him very dearly." She smiled sadly. "Just the way he'd been given to us."

CHAPTER 10

Not even at the height of the tourist season were so many people to be seen milling about Jupiter's Lookout at one time.

The murder area was in the process of being screened off and floodlit in readiness for the night which was closing in rapidly. The screening would give some protection from the sharp wind whistling across the cove, but there was little that could be done about keeping out the rain, at the moment little more than a fine, misty drizzle. With heavy showers and winds of up to Force Eight strength forecast for the next twenty-four hours, Detective-Inspector Donald Royal from the Sandycombe County Constabulary wouldn't be sorry when the police surgeon had finished with the body so that he could get on with his job.

At last the doctor stood up and said, "Not long. Two, maybe three hours. Sometime soon after lunch."

He looked down dispassionately at the murder victim; female; forty-five to fifty; lying curled up in the foetal position.

"You know who she is, don't you?" he said. "It's Edgar Kemp's younger daughter, Doris. You remember old Dr. Kemp."

Royal said he did and that George Parker, the local fisherman who had discovered the body on his way home around four o'clock that afternoon, had identified her for him.

"She crawled into that position to die, you know," said the doctor; a self-assured, bearded man in his late forties. "Some distance, I'd say, from where she was stabbed. You noticed her hands and finger-nails, I suppose?"

Royal said he had. He spoke abruptly. He didn't much care for the other man who was inclined to talk down to him. Perhaps unwittingly. But it was still irritating.

The doctor, whose name was McIntyre, got down on his

haunches again, then picked up one of the dead woman's hands and examined it closely. The palm was dirty; gritty; so were the finger-nails, two of which were torn and bloodied. Then he replaced the hand in the foetal curve of the body and stood up; dusted his own hand down the side of his raincoat.

"Well, that's my lot; I can do no more for now," he said. "I'll say good-night then."

Royal nodded; watched the doctor start down the cliff-path.

A young man of about thirty with a full head of prematurely grey hair and a thick, dark brown moustache came up to Royal and said, "They're coming up for her now." He looked down at the dead woman; shook his head slightly.

Royal understood the gesture. He too had felt unusually moved by the position the murder victim had taken up, possibly—as the doctor had suggested—while she had waited in the protective shelter of the boulder to die. A man of few words at the best of times, he made no comment.

The two men turned and followed the trail left in the muddy turf by the dying woman as she had clawed and dragged herself towards the boulder. It started behind the bench near the guard-rail and finished roughly a metre short of the boulder where Doris Kemp's strength had finally given out and she had curled up and died.

It was getting quite dark. The wind was growing steadily stronger. The two men paused near the bench where the trail began and crouched down over a wide semicircle of scratch marks in the wet ground. At the left-hand inner edge of the semicircle were two rather more distinctive scratch marks.

The young man with Royal, Detective-Sergeant William Spence angled his head to one side and said, "I make it double aitch."

Or an *A* and an *H*, thought Royal. The dying woman might have unwittingly partially obliterated the upper half of the *A* as she had dragged herself over to the boulder.

He looked up at the darkening sky; frowned. It was going to be a foul night. "We'll have to wait until morning for photographs and a plaster cast. It's too dark now. Better get something to cover this up before the rain washes everything away." He stood up. "The deceased mightn't have even known the letters were there. Soil and grit definitely would've got under her fingernails while she was dragging herself along. And that," he said, nodding at what had been scratched in the dirt, "looks to me as if it was done with some sharp-pointed instrument; a stick. Or the murder weapon itself; the point of a knife."

"Whoever killed her left us a cryptic clue to puzzle over; is that what you're saying?" The sergeant looked sceptical. "Bit theatrical, isn't it?"

"Ever meet the really dangerous nutter who wasn't? And that's what we're looking for here; a psycho," said Royal complacently, remembering how Doris Kemp had died. It didn't take much imagination to conjure up the maniacal frenzy her murderer must have worked himself into as he struck again and again with the knife he had used to kill her. "We'll have to see what the trick cyclists make of killers who leave cryptic messages with their victims for the police to find, won't we?"

Spence groaned. "God, I hate talking to psychiatrists."

Royal sighed inaudibly. "So you've said before."

It was blowing a gale and some fault in the street-lighting system had left the village in pitch darkness.

Mrs. Charles left the hotel and crossed the forecourt to the street. She had been waiting for over an hour to use the pay phone in the hall and had finally given up and decided to try the public one outside the George Hotel at the end of the street. First it had been the spritely pensioner who had reversed the charges and talked non-stop for almost twenty minutes. Her room was fantastic. The food was fantastic. The leisure facilities were fantastic. Everything—and she went through The Mermaid's virtues in exquisite detail—was *fan-tas-tic!* Then one of the younger guests, a boy of about twelve, had started playing noisily with the fruit machine right next to the phone; and lastly, the office, which had been vacated and locked up at eight, was suddenly reoccupied. By Penny, who rested her folded arms on the reception desk less than a metre away from the pay phone and idly watched the activities in the lounge through the thick glass partition wall opposite and looked set to remain that way indefinitely. Undoubtedly, all ears. There was no way Mrs. Charles could use the phone without the girl overhearing her conversation.

It took several attempts (and one lost coin) for the clairvoyante to get through to her brother.

"Cyril?" she asked hesitantly as his thin voice quavered uncertainly down an extremely muzzy line. The tree beside the telephone kiosk threshed about wildly, its wet branches scraping against the glass. She raised her voice. "It's 'Del here. I'm a little short of small change so listen carefully. I want you to check up on somebody for me. A woman. I won't go into all the details now, Cyril, but she was in panto with you in the West End one time. The woman who played the part of Tweedledee. You introduced me to her back-stage one afternoon without giving me her real name."

There was a long pause; complete, deathly silence.

"Are you still there, Cyril?" Mrs. Charles inquired.

"Yes. I'm thinking. I can't remember her name. But I know somebody from those days who might."

"But you do remember her?"

Another very long pause. Then: "Yes."

"Good. Find out all you can about her and then phone me back at The Mermaid. I'll give you the number of the pay phone there. I specifically don't want your call to go through the hotel's switchboard. Have you got that?"

She paused and quickly inserted another coin.

"You're still there?" she asked. "Good. Now, whatever you do, *don't* leave a message. If I'm not in, phone again."

Cyril said, "Have you been over to Sandycombe and visited Harry?"

"No, not yet. I thought I might do that over the week-end. Sandycombe is holding a soap-box derby on Sunday and I thought it might be interesting to go over there and watch the race. I'll think about seeing Harry then. I'll give him your kind regards; that's if you've changed your mind about coming down."

Cyril kept a silent counsel.

"I'll have to ring off now, Cyril. I'm out of change. Are you quite sure you've got the right person? Tweedledee. The little fluffy-haired woman who twirls about a lot."

Cyril assured her he had and took down the number she gave him; then, to the accompaniment of the warning pips, they said good-bye and rang off.

The clairvoyante awoke with a start. Somebody had screamed.

She groped for the light switch and looked at the time by her wrist-watch. Six thirty-five. She got quickly out of bed and went to the window. She couldn't be sure, but it had seemed to her that the scream had come from somewhere outside rather than inside the hotel.

Parting the curtains a little, she looked out. Standing near the pool-side in the grey, early morning light with her hands to her face was the swimmer whom Mrs. Charles had seen in the pool during the day of her arrival at The Mermaid. She was wearing a bathing costume and backless, medium-heeled sandals. A white bath towel was held in the crook of her right arm.

Lying facedown on the bottom of the pool was another female; fully clothed but shoeless. A pair of white, stiletto-heeled sling-backs had been left neatly beside the ladder attached to the side of the pool.

The chef suddenly appeared; the swimmer pointed. He looked; without a word whipped off his blue and white striped apron and shed his shoes and dived straight into the water. At that moment Tony Murdoch, in his breakfast waiter's outfit, appeared on the scene and spoke to the woman; then, as the chef surfaced, responded quickly to his call for assistance. The chef heaved and Tony Murdoch dragged. The woman in the bathing costume watched spellbound with horror as a teenaged girl was laid out on the tiled pool-surround and the chef got down quickly on all fours and bent over her. He could see it was too late, but he nevertheless cupped her small, pointed face in his hands and tried to blow air into her mouth.

Liza Murdoch came running out just as he was getting back on his feet. She looked down at the drowned girl.

"My God," Mrs. Charles heard her say. "It's Dee. She's not—?"

Nobody answered her.

"How did it happen?" asked Liza. "Did anyone see her fall in?"

The chef looked questioningly at the swimmer who shook her head numbly.

"Better get a blanket," said Tony Murdoch quickly. "Will you take care of it please, Liza?"

His wife nodded; backed up a few steps, then turned and hurried away.

"I'll phone the police as soon as Liza comes back," said Tony Murdoch to no one in particular. Then, to the chef: "You'd better change into some dry clothes and get back to the kitchen." He looked at the swimmer. "I'd appreciate it if you didn't have anything to say about this to the other guests for the present."

The clairvoyante let the curtains fall softly back into place.

She had just finished dressing when there was a light tap on her door. She paused to gather up the room key and her handbag before answering it. Then, opening the door wide, she smiled and said good-morning to the dark-haired girl with the *"Hi, I'm Josie"* brooch pinned to her frilly pink nylon blouse who waited without.

Josie returned the greeting but not the smile. She looked pale and seemed in a rush, as if she had more important business to attend to elsewhere. She barely delivered the full message that there was an urgent telephone call waiting for Mrs. Charles on the extension phone in reception before hurrying off.

Frowning, Mrs. Charles closed the door behind her and followed Josie along the corridor and into the hall. How typical of Cyril to forget her instructions about phoning her back. No doubt he had lost the number she had given him. He'd probably never even bothered to take it down!

Before speaking into the phone, Mrs. Charles glanced across the desk at Josie who was preparing that day's menus. The girl took no notice of her and went on with what she was doing.

"Cyril?" said Mrs. Charles.

"It's Courtney Harrington here, 'Del," an anxious voice responded. "Thank goodness I've caught you. I was afraid you might've gone out. Can you speak freely?"

"No, not really," she replied, smiling at Josie when the girl glanced up at her briefly.

"Well, in that case I think you'd better drop round and see me. As soon as you can. I'd come to you only I've an idea that it could lead to complications. For both of us."

"I'll be with you in about an hour; as soon as I've had breakfast," the clairvoyante promised; and rang off.

Two men, one tall, about fifty, and wearing a green and fawn check hat, the other younger, moustachioed, grey-haired and hatless, excused themselves as they squeezed past her in the narrow hall.

Mrs. Charles glanced at the girl behind the desk. Josie's face was frozen; mask like. She made no response to the curt nod the hatted man gave her; merely watched the men's progress past the desk and down the hall.

Police, guessed the clairvoyante; and went in to breakfast.

CHAPTER 11

The swami's hand was unsteady as he poured tea for his visitor and himself.

"I'm shaking like a leaf," he said unnecessarily. "I haven't felt so scared since—" He frowned. "Well, that's another story."

"Then the sooner you get it off your chest," said Mrs. Charles calmly, "the better you'll feel."

He nodded and took a deep breath. "Early this morning," he began, "I slipped down to the quay to pick up some fish. I do that first thing every Wednesday morning: I get it fresh—cheap too—from a friend of mine down there. And they, the men who work on the boats and around the quay handling the fish," he went on after pausing to take another deep breath, "were all talking about it. One of them stumbled across a woman's body on the cliffs yesterday afternoon. She'd been stabbed to death; savagely murdered. The work of a crazy person; a fiend," he murmured distractedly. "Somebody local too, they're saying down on the quay. That's the awful part about it. The murder weapon hasn't come to light yet, but the story going round is that the police are looking for a special kind of knife, like the sort a fisherman might use to gut fish."

"This woman; who was she? Do you know?"

He nodded quickly; took a clean white handkerchief from the pocket of his grey cardigan and held it momentarily to his lips, then pressed it against either side of his face and under his chin. "A close friend of Peggy and Albert May's by the name of Kemp; Doris Kemp," he replied.

The clairvoyante sighed deeply. "Oh, dear; I'm very sorry to hear that. I was only talking to her yesterday too; shortly before lunch."

"I know, I know," said the swami, dismayed. His hand shook badly as he raised his cup to his lips and a drop or two of tea splashed into the saucer. He drank noisily, swallowing in large, nervous gulps. "And it won't be long before the police know it too." He was speaking indistinctly through the handkerchief which was again pressed to his lips. He held it there for a moment longer. Then, taking it away: "The description the woman —some kind of witness—gave the police was of you, 'Del. It matched you in every detail—well, almost: near enough for me to guess who it was. This witness told the police she saw you—a fairhaired woman in a beige cloak—and Doris Kemp together up on the cliffs. Apparently you paused for several moments near the bench up there at Jupiter's Lookout where this woman (the witness) was resting; then you continued on to what, from her description, was obviously Albert and Peggy May's cottage and Doris Kemp came out and let you in."

"Do you know the name of this witness?"

He shook his head. "I only know that she's a visitor to Michaelmas Cove; like yourself."

Mrs. Charles sipped her tea. Tweedledee again. Not so daft as she looked. Or pretended to be.

The swami mopped his sweaty brow, then dabbed the handkerchief nervously backwards and forwards across his smooth and shiny scalp. "The folk down on the quay are saying that there was a message scratched in the path near Doris Kemp's body. The initials, everyone seems to think, of her killer's name. Double aitch; or an *A* and an aitch."

Mrs. Charles widened her eyes. "Adele Herrmann?"

The old man was beginning to look quite ill. He groaned a little. "I don't know how you can take it all so calmly, 'Del. You can see the state I'm in. I don't know whether I'm Arthur or Martha! This wretched place has destroyed me and now it's your turn. You know there are evil influences here, 'Del. You can't afford to be complacent. Be warned. Get out while there's still time. You're walking into the same trap I did."

"I think not, Courtney," she said quietly.

He wagged his head sadly at her. Then, after a moment, he

said, "I'm almost afraid to ask you this, 'Del. What name did Doris Kemp know you by? Your real name; or the one you told me you're using at the moment, Edwina Charles?"

"My maiden name."

The dismayed expression on the swami's face betrayed that this was what he had feared. He made a small, deprecative noise. Then: "The police think her killer left her for dead. In other words, whoever killed her didn't realise she was still alive, just, and able to leave a clue to his identity. George Parker, the man who found her, told me her hands and finger-nails looked as if she'd been scratching in the dirt."

The clairvoyante regarded him with some interest. "Whyever would Doris Kemp leave my initials on the path, Courtney? I didn't kill her. Unless—" She paused and gazed over the swami's head at the leafy fronds of the potted fern on the tall plant stand behind his chair. Then, musingly: "Let's assume for the moment that Doris Kemp *did* scratch my initials in the dirt. Was she directing the police to me not as her murderer but as the person who knows who did kill her? We talked a lot about Peggy and Albert May and some other people, and very possibly someone or something that we discussed might've suddenly awakened some half-forgotten memory. In which case," she murmured abstractedly, as if alone and talking to herself, "I wonder if I'm nearer to the truth than I think I am."

She lowered her gaze so that she was looking directly now at the swami. "I confess that after talking to Doris Kemp yesterday, I felt that certain aspects of the situation were showing definite signs of proving hopeless. And I do not accept or admit defeat easily."

The clairvoyante was quiet for a moment, thinking back carefully over her visit to Albert and Peggy May's cottage. Her eyes narrowed. That harsh metallic clicking sound as the flap over the mail-slot snapped shut . . . In any other circumstances she would have accepted without question Doris Kemp's explanation that the flap had a habit of sticking when children had been playing about with it. But not in this instance. Somebody had been there on the porch watching them through the mail-slot and listening to their conversation . . .

The swami broke in on her thoughts. "But if Doris Kemp *didn't* leave your initials there, who did? Have you wondered about that?"

Mrs. Charles gazed at the fern for quite some while before answering him.

"Yes, Courtney," she replied at length. "It so happens I have asked myself that question." She looked straight into his eyes and smiled gravely. "Some other person who knows me as Adele Herrmann?"

He started violently forward in his chair, almost sending his cup and saucer flying. *"Me?* You're not thinking it was me? Bless me, bless my soul; *no,* 'Del! Not me. I swear it!"

"Your nerves are in a frightful state, Courtney," she remarked evenly. "Doris Kemp's killer knows nothing about Edwina Charles."

He blinked stupidly at her. Then his expression cleared. "Of course! Why would I use *AH* when, as you told me yesterday as you were leaving, everyone here knows you as Edwina, Mrs. Charles?"

They lapsed into a thoughtful silence. The swami was the first to speak again.

"We've got him," he announced.

"I'm glad you think so, Courtney. Unfortunately I am unable to share your optimism. I personally can't see that I am any nearer to the truth about what is wrong here in Michaelmas Cove than I was before Doris Kemp was murdered."

"But we know that the person who killed her is somebody like me; somebody from the past."

The clairvoyante shook her head. "Not necessarily." She then went on to relate the incident with the metal flap on the Mays' mail-slot and told him what she suspected. "And if I'm right," she continued, "and there was somebody eavesdropping on our conversation, then that could be where her killer got hold of the name Adele Herrmann. He overheard Doris Kemp using it." She smiled wryly. "He could be in for the shock of his life when he discovers that everybody in Michaelmas Cove—with the exception of yourself, that is—addresses me by a quite different name."

"Ah," he said, wagging a warning finger at her, "but it wouldn't be too difficult to correct his mistake, would it? All it would take is an anonymous phone call to the police letting them know that you (the Mrs. Edwina Charles staying at The Mermaid) are the mysterious *AH*."

She nodded thoughtfully. "I find that aspect of this whole unfortunate affair most intriguing. If Doris Kemp's killer deliberately left my initials scratched on the path to incriminate me in her murder, what will he do when he discovers his mistake? Correct it in the manner you've suggested?" Her eyebrows rose interrogatively. "Find some other way around his dilemma?" *Or leave well enough alone and avoid the risk of compounding his mistake?* she wondered privately.

The distressed look on the swami's face suggested that were he in her shoes, he would not wait around to find out: his bags would be packed and he would be gone long before the police came knocking on *his* door. He sighed to himself. If only he had one tenth of her courage things would have been so different. He gazed at her admiringly. She was a most remarkable woman. He had never met anyone quite like her. Truly gifted; quite unique . . .

The clairvoyante's voice cut across his thoughts.

"Two of the people Doris Kemp and I discussed yesterday were Pearl Farrow and her mother." Her eyes narrowed. "Tell me more about them, Courtney. Everything you know."

He frowned. "What sort of thing do you want to know?"

"Anything. I don't care how trivial it is."

His frown deepened as he gazed at some spot above her head. Then, widening his eyes and looking straight at her: "There's nothing more to tell. I've told you everything I know. I hardly know them, 'Del. In fact, I don't think I've ever spoken to either one of them; Mary Farrow *or* Pearl. Mary Farrow is a bit funny about men; crosses to the other side of the road quick as a flash when she spots a male walking towards her. At least, that's what she's always done when she's seen me heading her way. And yet . . ." He paused; thought for a moment. Then: "That makes her sound timid, as if she's terrified of me; and maybe she is. But that's only part of it, I'm sure of that. She's a Man-hater. Capital letters! I cornered her once, left her no retreat, no means of escape. Not deliberately, of course: it was just one of those things that often happen in these narrow lanes of ours. And the look she gave me when we eventually passed one another!" He shook his head slowly. "*Malevolent*. Yes, that's the word for it. She could have killed me! I admit that it might've been because she was trapped, so to speak." He thought about it for a few moments. Then, with a frown: "What are you going to tell the police when and if they eventually get round to you, 'Del?"

"Very probably nothing at all. I can't prove any of my suspicions, only make things look bad for myself."

"Does this mean you think Doris Kemp's murder is linked with Peggy May's suicide?"

"Doris Kemp was murdered because she had talked to me. I only wish there could be some other explanation for it, but I fear there isn't. Doris Kemp had to be silenced. She was a threat; not, I believe, because of what she knew, but because of what she might remember. I'm positive that subconsciously Doris Kemp held the key to everything that has occurred here in recent months."

The swami sighed. "Well, I certainly wish I knew what it's all about. I feel as if I'm sitting on a powder keg, one that's had its fuse lit! I remember talking to somebody once—this was when I was living in a big town; before I moved down here. I forget now what the lady's problem was (she was a client of mine), but it was all tied up with something unpleasant that had happened in her past . . . when she was living in a small place like this. As she got up to leave one day, she suddenly paused and turned back to me with the comment that people thought life was all in the big cities and towns. But this wasn't so, she said. Then she said she'd willingly defy any city or town dweller to match the goings-on of the sleepy-looking country village. '*Stranger than fiction*'; that was her way of describing it. And after having myself lived in a village now for quite a few years, I'd say that if anything, that was an understatement."

There was a small pause; then Mrs. Charles said, "While we're on the subject of fiction, I called on Mrs. Claythorpe yesterday afternoon and she gave me her version of Fr. Thomas' fall down the cliffs. She claims someone pushed him over the edge. She also said he gave her a gentle warning not to spread it about."

The swami looked at her and his eyes grew big and round. "I know she wouldn't have it that he fell accidentally, but that's the first anyone's ever said to me about his having warned her to watch her tongue. That doesn't sound a bit like him."

"Could there be anything in it?"

"Why would anyone want to push Fr. Thomas over the cliffs?" He shrugged a little. "I suppose it's possible that somebody with a fetish about monks, somebody who was cruelly treated by the holy fathers when he was a lad, or something of the kind, took it out on him. But I hardly think so."

"No, it wouldn't seem very likely," agreed Mrs. Charles. She smiled faintly. "I seem to be walking around in a circle. In the centre of which—?" She widened her eyes at the swami and he slowly shook his head.

"It's no good asking me; I don't know what you're looking for, 'Del."

The colour of the clairvoyante's eyes darkened as she concentrated her gaze on him. "I was about to say that I don't know either. But that's not strictly true. I know *who* is in the centre of the circle; I had the answer to that twenty-five years ago. What I don't know is *why*."

CHAPTER 12

Royal was tired; in no mood for playing games. Not the kind Josie May wanted to play. A tease, the chef had called her. He had sounded piqued, probably with some justification. (There was no reason to suppose that she hadn't led him on at some time: all men were fair game to her kind.) But Royal thought he had detected something else in the man's attitude towards her. Over and above his wounded masculine pride, that is. While it seemed more than likely that the chef had lusted after the girl, deep down the same man didn't really like her. Neither did Royal. Some girls got into trouble; this one made it.

They were in the Murdochs' private sitting-room on the first floor, Liza Murdoch having managed to prise Mrs. Murdoch, Sr., from the easy chair near the gas fire. Royal was standing with his back to the window which overlooked the internal courtyard and the swimming-pool; the girl was sitting on the sofa with her legs crossed and her hands folded loosely in her lap.

Wearily, Royal looked at her and said, "Mr. Jeffreys, the chef, told me that you and Deanna Bastian were close friends."

"I knew her," said Josie evenly.

"Well enough to make the statement to Mr. Jeffreys that she had committed suicide," said Royal.

"Didn't she?" the girl asked coolly.

"You obviously have some reason for thinking so."

Josie gazed steadily at Royal. Then, inclining her head at the door behind her, she said, "Ask her."

"Ask who what, Miss May?"

"Mrs. Murdoch," she replied after a moment. "Ask her if Dee committed suicide. It was her old man Dee was having it off with."

Royal stared at her. "Are you saying the dead girl was having an affair with her employer?"

The girl looked at him coldly. Then, in an insolent drawl: "Ronnie is what I said; Mrs. Murdoch's ex. Or that's what he's supposed to be. We've only got her ladyship's word for it that she and Tony Murdoch are really married, haven't we?"

He folded his arms and leaned back on his heels. "Ronnie who?" he asked resignedly.

"I've really no idea. I've already told you. Ask *her*." The dark head tilted at the door again. "Or Dee's mother. She should know his name. He calls often enough at her shop."

"In other words Deanna's mother was aware of her relationship with this man, Ronnie?"

"In other words," said the girl with a small, faintly patronising smile, "Ronnie's a sales rep. And if Mrs. Bastian can't help you with a name, you might try Mrs. Farrow. Another of Ronnie's friends," she added dryly.

"Farrow," said Royal thoughtfully, trying to remember where he had heard the name.

"Pearl Farrow's mother." Josie gave him a quizzical look. "St. Pearl of the cliffs?"

Ah yes, thought Royal. Now he remembered. That strange business about the old priest who took a nasty tumble down the cliffs from Jupiter's Lookout after having had one too many. Never really got to the bottom of it . . .

Josie went on, "I don't think Dee realised what a busy man our Ronnie is. Dee must've been waiting for him at Jupiter's Lookout and when he didn't turn up, she started back down again and met up with him outside Mrs. Farrow's place. Anyway," she said offhandedly, "that was where I saw them together. Right outside the Farrows' front door. Of course, I could be wrong."

Royal looked at her.

The girl's eyes laughed at him. "Maybe Ronnie'd suddenly got religion and had stopped off at the Farrows' on pilgrimage."

Royal studied her distastefully. Some of what she was saying was true; a lot of it wasn't; and the longer he talked to her, the bolder and more malefic she would become. And for no other purpose that he could see than to make trouble for as many people as she could. Including the police. She was what his young son would call *"a sicko."*

"Did Deanna ever mention suicide specifically to you?" he asked.

"No, she was too scared."

"Scared of what?"

"That everyone would find out about her and Ronnie, of course," she said smoothly. "Specially her father. He's a heavy drinker and gets pretty violent when he's had too much. Dee was terrified of him."

Oh Lord, thought Royal. I asked for that! Now she's dragged in the father. And how many other people before he was through with her?

He decided to terminate the interview. Before the girl could turn what was probably a routine suicide investigation into a major indictment of everyone who had ever crossed her. She would have the memory of an elephant. Antagonise her and you'd have an enemy for life. Not a pleasant thought.

"That was Josie May who just came out, wasn't it?" asked Sergeant Spence a few minutes later as he followed Royal downstairs.

"You know her?" inquired Royal over his shoulder.

"I've seen her around. I knew her brother, Felix." Spence grinned. "Felix May used to work for his uncle Albert—you know, the smuggler—until he passed on."

"That a fact?" said Royal. He glanced back at Spence. "I always thought that smuggling rumour was only a story put round by the Mays to frighten little children. Felix not interested in keeping the old family business going?"

"Dunno," said Spence. "The last I heard he'd drifted up North to the oilfields looking for work. This was after some local popsy tossed him over for another bloke."

Royal looked at him sharply and a piece of the puzzle slotted into place. That was if the name of the girl who had jilted Josie May's brother was Deanna Bastian.

They reached the half-landing and started down the next flight of steps.

"You know very well that Albert May was a smuggler," said the sergeant with another grin.

"I know nothing of the sort," said Royal.

The sergeant's grin widened. "Your secret is safe with me, sir. My lips are sealed."

Royal smiled at him and the sergeant said, "McIntyre's been on the blower. He's not in a very good mood and wants to know which one you want done first. The stabbing or the drowning?"

"Since when has what I want made any difference to McIntyre? He'll suit himself whatever I say. He thinks he knows best, anyhow. How did you make out with the other girl—Penny whatever-her-name-is?"

"Reynolds. It looks like we could have another ouija board suicide on our hands. According to Penny that's how Deanna got it into her head to commit suicide by drowning. Penny reckons the idea was deliberately planted there and that Deanna would never have thought of it by herself."

Royal paused on the stairs and looked at him. "Jesus," he said disgustedly.

"Penny said Deanna was very upset after they'd been messing about with a ouija board last Sunday night. It was a threesome. Josie May, Penny Reynolds and Deanna Bastian. From what I can gather, Josie May did most of the talking and made some prediction—or said something (I'm not sure which it was)—which scared the living daylights out of Deanna. Penny's been pretty badly shaken up by what's happened and I thought it best if we talked to her again later; after she's had time to calm down a bit."

Royal nodded and stepped down into the hall. "I'm off up the cliffs," he said.

"There was nothing doing up there the last time I checked," said the sergeant. "It could be weeks before the murder weapon turns up. If at all. That's if it was tossed over the cliffs into the sea."

"And maybe it was back at work again this morning gutting fish down on the quay," said Royal.

"Charming," said the sergeant. "Mr. Bastian wants to know when he and his wife can see their daughter."

"Later; when McIntyre's finished with her."

"Want me to tell them; or shall I send a W.P.C. round?"

"You go. And while you're about it, don't ask any direct questions, but sniff around and see what you can find out. Oh, and I wouldn't go mentioning the ouija board just yet awhile. Wait until you've had another word with young Penny what's-it."

"Anything specific in mind?"

"Just a thought. I've an idea McIntyre might be going to tell us the girl was pregnant."

As they moved up the hall, Royal said, "If you're looking for me I'll be calling at the Farrows' on my way up to Jupiter's Lookout."

"Crikey," said the sergeant, grinning. "Things must really be getting desperate if we've got to consult the oracle!"

The elderly woman standing outside the shop continued to bang on the glass and rattle the doorknob. She had read the hastily scrawled notice, *Closed due to a bereavement in the family;* but what about her bread? She had a regular standing order, and the bread man had been; she had seen him making his delivery soon after eight. It would only take Agnes Bastian a few seconds to give her her bread; otherwise she would have to traipse all the way over to the supermarket in Tebbit Street and they didn't have the sort she liked; the sliced, crusty loaf . . .

Agnes Bastian was crying. "You see to it, Jack," she said to her husband.

"Bloody hell!" he exclaimed angrily. "You'd think they'd have the decency not to trouble us today. Some people are selfish swine."

"It could be the police again," said his wife.

Jack Bastian, a small, balding man with an aggressive manner, drunk or sober, swore and started down the stairs.

His wife listened to him clomp-clomp heavily all the way to the bottom: then she left the kitchen and went into her daughter's room. She stood in the middle of it, one thought running con-

stantly through her mind, *I don't believe it; I don't believe it;*
over and over again.

She could hear her husband's voice drifting up from the shop
below; a woman talking at the same time, neither listening to nor
remotely interested in what he was having to say. Old Mrs. Poole
after her bread . . .

Absently, Dee's mother winkled out a small pile of lacy
French knickers from beneath the jumble of paperbacks and
magazines scattered across a painted wicker chair near the window and put them in the top left-hand drawer of the dressing-table, pausing and frowning at the nearly empty packet of sanitary
napkins squashed up at the back. The packet hadn't been
touched first thing yesterday morning when she had put some
clean handkerchiefs in there; and it was a little early yet for Dee's
period, wasn't it?

Still frowning, Agnes Bastian crossed to the bed, felt about
under the pillow, then changed her mind. It was a waste of time
looking at the calendar in Dee's diary. It was one of those silly
little ones with the months running across the page instead of
down it; and somehow she always got confused and counted one
week too few when she used that kind of calendar.

She went back to the kitchen and ran a forefinger over the
boldly inked tradesman's calendar pinned to the back of the
door; found the small mark she had made last month; counted
the weeks.

Odd.

Dee wasn't due until the day after tomorrow . . .

Reluctantly, Mary Farrow admitted the plain clothes detective to
her home.

She was a plain woman, fifty-two years old, of average height
and build but with an air of wiry strength about her. And rather
tense-looking, thought Royal. The almost ankle-length dark
brown woollen dress she was wearing, the height of fashion in the
twenties, drooped lifelessly from her square shoulders and gave
her no shape at all. Royal was even moved to wonder if she were
wearing the old-fashioned binders of the same period as her dress

to keep her chest schoolboy flat. Her fine, mousy-brown hair was scraped back harshly from her face into a small twist in the nape of her neck. He noted, though, that the hair crinkled where it was drawn back from her temples which suggested that if it were to receive less severe treatment, it would probably be very soft and pretty, and may have even gone a long way towards redeeming her otherwise drab features. All round, he decided, she was about the most mannish-looking female (deliberately, he suspected) he'd ever laid eyes on. A right turn off!

As if suddenly more keenly aware of the differences in their sex and the fact that she was under male scrutiny, Mary Farrow drew well back from him until she merged with the dark furniture and the old-fashioned brown paintwork in the gloomy hall.

"You'd better go on into the front room," she said in a flat, colourless voice.

A young girl in a pair of blue denim dungarees and a bright yellow Mickey Mouse tee-shirt sat near a cheerless coal fire working at a jigsaw puzzle. She did not look up as her mother and the man entered the room.

"Pearl will be wanting her lunch," said Mary Farrow tonelessly. "I've only got a minute."

"This shouldn't take long, Mrs. Farrow," said Royal politely. "It's about a man." He smiled apologetically. "I'm sorry, I only have his Christian name, Ronnie; but I believe he's a friend of yours. A young woman who's been helping us with our inquiries into a tragic incident which occurred in the village early this morning has told us she saw him outside your front door on one occasion. She admitted that he could've been a pilgrim, but she rather seemed to think he might've been a personal friend."

Mary Farrow was standing very erect with her hands clasped tightly in front of her. There was a stern expression on her face—like that, thought Royal, of a spinster school-marm who was about to reprimand a naughty pupil. He half expected to be told to hold out his hand and then become the hapless recipient of six of the best!

"There's no man-friend visiting in my home. Not now, not yesterday, not ever! I'll have no truck with men. And I'll have the law on anyone who says different! Malicious, it is, to say things like that about decent self-respecting folk like me. I'll have none of it, you hear! Nobody's got a right to go around casting a slur on my good name."

Royal's eyes lingered on the girl sitting quite motionless by the fireplace, her bowed head no more than fifteen centimetres above the puzzle on which she was concentrating so intently.

As if sensing that she were under observation, the girl suddenly raised her head and gazed past the stranger through the open doorway to the dark hall beyond. Royal was oddly touched by her lack of response: he couldn't help feeling that as she did not know the stranger in the room, for her he simply did not exist.

After a moment, the girl looked back at the puzzle and bent her head over it again. It was the first time that Royal had seen Pearl Farrow at close quarters, and now that he had, he still didn't know what to make of her. Did anyone? What went on inside that head of hers? Was she really clairvoyant? Or had she just made a lucky guess? Maybe it would never happen again. She wouldn't be the first clairvoyant to enjoy a blaze of publicity and then fade into obscurity, never hitting the jackpot with another correct prediction again for as long as she lived.

"I'm sorry," said Royal, looking back at Mary Farrow. "There's obviously been some mistake. Please accept my sincere apologies. You'll hear no more about the matter, I assure you."

Mary Farrow saw him to the door. Her farewell was a warning.

"You tell that woman, whoever she is, I'll have the law on her for spreading malicious gossip about me. Telling people that I've got a man about the place . . . I won't have it, you hear!"

Royal raised his hat politely and said, "Good-morning: I'm so sorry you were troubled, Mrs. Farrow," and left it at that. The least said the better. He hadn't really thought she would know "Ronnie," but it had been worth a try. Anything—even confronting that old dragon in her lair—was better than further distressing the dead girl's parents, or embarrassing Liza Murdoch, with what he had suspected from the outset was basically a vindictive piece of mischief-making. Josie May was paying Deanna back for having hurt her brother, Felix; and she'd go on paying her back. It wasn't enough for her that the poor girl was dead. She wouldn't be satisfied until she'd torn the girl's memory, her reputation, to shreds.

Suicide? Like hell it was! Josie May killed Deanna Bastian. With a ouija board.

He wondered grimly what his chances would be of making the charge stick.

CHAPTER 13

"Is that you, 'Del?"

Cyril Forbes' voice crackled indistinctly down the line.

"Yes, Cyril," replied his sister. "Speak up a little, will you? I can barely hear you." She had just come in from the street when the call came through for her and hadn't had time to take off her jacket and headscarf.

Her brother raised his voice. "I found out about her; the woman you wanted me to check up on."

"Yes, Cyril."

There was a long silence during which the clairvoyante unknotted the scarf and withdrew it from her head.

"Well, Cyril?" she said at length, very patiently. She hoped she was not going to have to begin this conversation all over again. It was not impossible.

"Yes," said Cyril.

"Yes *what*, Cyril?" she asked, and sighed to herself. This was going to be difficult after all. Cyril was obviously having one of his "days" and would therefore need constant prompting to keep him from wandering off the subject. And that made things rather awkward. Someone—*Hi, I'm Josie*, Mrs. Charles was inclined to think—was hovering in the corridor which led from the hall to the annex where the deluxe rooms were located. Perhaps quite innocently. The clairvoyante wasn't sure.

"I thought you'd find that very interesting," said Cyril.

Mrs. Charles sighed to herself. The conversation she had hoped he would have with her, he had had with himself, inside his head.

"In what way, Cyril?" she inquired.

She could almost hear her brother frown—the way he always

did when she failed to grasp what he was talking about. The line crackled noisily as he replied. "Hamburger," he said. There was a lot more static interference, then she caught another two words which sounded something like "badly burnt." Her eyes widened. She must be going mad! How on earth had a badly burnt hamburger got into this conversation?

"Forgive me, Cyril," she said gravely. "This is a very bad line. Would you mind repeating what you just said?"

"Bridger," he said. Then, shouting: "BRIDGER!"

"Oh," she said. "Yes, I know who you mean now. I'm sorry, Cyril: I thought I heard you say something quite different."

"No," he said. "Bridger is what I said . . . The fellow who ran the concert party Peggy Baldwin was in. Bam Bridger."

Mrs. Charles quickly held the receiver away from her ear as the line gave an agonised high-pitched squeal. She thought she had heard her brother correctly but wanted to be quite sure. "*Ham*, you said?" she asked when the line quietened down again.

"No, 'Del!" (Cyril was becoming just a little impatient.) "*Bam*. B-A-M!" he shouted. "Bridger's real name is Bambridge, or Bembridge; something like that. You know what some of these entertainers are like: they change their names to something they think'll be easier for the public to remember and will look good on the handbill."

"I see," said his sister.

There was another long silence. Then Mrs. Charles said, "I'm sorry to be so dull-witted this evening, Cyril; but why should I find him so interesting when I already know about him?"

"Who told you?" he demanded.

Oh, dear, thought Mrs. Charles. *Oh, dearie, dearie me!* "Told me what, Cyril?"

"Who told you about Bridger and that woman you asked about?"

Mrs. Charles closed her eyes for a moment. Then she took a very deep breath and said, "Now, I want you to be very patient with me, Cyril. This is an extremely bad line and I've got a bit of a headache tonight. I'm not thinking at all clearly. You must bear with me. I think it would be a good idea if we talked this over when you come down on Saturday. That's if you're still coming. You can tell me all about it then."

"There's nothing more to tell," he said. "She was in Bridger's concert party for a time. Not for very long. She wasn't much of a dancer, and she had a voice that'd grate raw carrots. She was on Bridger's books," said Cyril very distinctly. "She worked for his agency."

"Yes, I understand now," said his sister. "That's all very interesting," she added.

"That's what I said." There was a further pause and the clairvoyante heard her brother frown again. "You're very vague tonight, 'Del," he complained. "You don't seem to be following me at all well."

"No," she said, smiling a little. "It's very difficult over the phone. Especially with a bad line."

She turned suddenly at the sound of footsteps and watched Josie unlock the office, without looking round at her, and disappear. The girl was carrying some menus in one hand, and tucked under her other arm was a folded newspaper.

"Are you still there, 'Del?" Cyril asked.

"Yes, I'm here," she responded.

There was a lengthy silence.

"What are you thinking, 'Del?"

"A lot of things, Cyril."

Another silence.

" 'Del?"

"Yes, Cyril."

"You be careful."

"I will, Cyril; I promise you that. I'll meet you at the coach station in Sandycombe on Saturday if you like." There was no direct coach service from St. Ives to Michaelmas Cove at weekends, and only three times during the week. Cyril was going to have to travel to Sandycombe and then take the bus.

He promised he would be there. She made him repeat after her the arrangements for their meeting at the week-end and then rang off.

He probably wouldn't turn up.

As Mrs. Charles walked away from the pay phone, Liza Murdoch came out of the lounge and crossed the hall to the office.

"Everything all right?" she asked with a fixed smile. She did not expect an answer and had disappeared into the office before there was time for Mrs. Charles to respond anyway.

Josie turned round from the desk as Liza closed the door. Liza looked fraught and Josie wondered if she had been fighting with the old battleaxe upstairs again. Josie hoped she wasn't going to be bored with all the details of their latest barney. It really got on her wick . . .

Josie reached under the desk for her shoulder-bag. Liza was leaning over the typewriter reading Josie's newspaper—a copy of the *Sandycombe Express*. Josie watched her for a moment without speaking. Then, when it looked as though Liza might have finished reading the article on the bitterly opposed supplementary council rate the already heavily financially burdened Michaelmas Cove ratepayer was going to be expected to fund over the next twelve months, Josie said, "She was a friend of my aunt's."

Liza looked up quickly. "Who? Oh—" she glanced down again at the paper "—the woman who was murdered up on the cliffs yesterday afternoon." She gazed at the photograph of Doris Kemp; a much younger woman than the one Mrs. Charles had talked with at the Mays' cottage the previous day. "Did you know her?" Liza picked up the newspaper and sat down with it on the typist's chair.

"Only slightly. Felix—my brother—knew her better than I did. But that was because he worked for my uncle Albert on his boat —my aunt's husband." Josie paused; waited for Liza to read the full report of the killing. After a moment, she moved up and stood beside Liza looking over her shoulder at the paper.

"It's her in twelve, isn't it?" Josie said.

Liza looked up. "Sorry, I wasn't listening. What did you say?"

Josie repeated herself; adding, "The woman the police want to interview. Tall, attractive, blonde, her age, and wearing a beige cloak. I saw the cloak this morning when I went to her room before breakfast to call her to the phone. The bathroom door was open and I could see it hanging from the shower-rose over the bath. Y'know, as if it'd got soaking wet and she was leaving it there to drip-dry."

Liza frowned. She remembered the cloak. Mrs. Charles had had it on the day she'd arrived. And she'd been wearing it when she went out yesterday morning. But not at all today. Twice Liza had seen her; and both times she had been wearing a fur-trimmed suede jacket.

Liza looked at the door as if hoping to find someone standing there who would be prepared to shoulder this particular burden for her.

"You don't really think it could be her, Mrs. Charles, do you?" she asked Josie.

"Of course it's her."

Liza looked at Josie. Then, glancing at the door again and frowning: "Leave this for Tony to handle." She looked back at the girl. "Don't you go talking to the police, will you?"

"*Me* talk to the police?" Josie laughed scornfully. "You must be joking! I've had a right basinful of them today. You can do what you like about her; *I* couldn't care less. I'm off home."

Josie slung her bag over her shoulder and held out her hand. "The *Express*," she said. "It's Mum's. She'll murder me if I forget to bring it home with me after her phoning up specially to remind me to get a copy so she can read all about Miss Kemp. Mum met her a few times at my uncle's place."

Liza wasn't listening. "Had it been—?" She hesitated; frowned. "D'you think Mrs. Charles' cloak had been washed?"

"To get rid of some bloodstains, you mean?" Josie lingered over the question as if the thought had not occurred to her. "Could be. Why not? See you," she said breezily, and went out of the door.

Liza watched her leave. She felt torn. She knew when she was being used. And that Josie was a born trouble-maker. But the fact remained that Mrs. Edwina Charles of Room 12 fitted to a tee the description given in the *Express* of the woman the Sandycombe police wished to interview.

Liza went thoughtfully out of the office; locked it up behind her. She'd better tell Tony. But she wouldn't mention anything about Josie. She'd simply say that she'd read the *Express* she'd found lying about the office and that she thought the unidentified woman the police wanted to interview in connection with yesterday's murder might be Mrs. Charles and leave it at that. Tony couldn't stand Josie; would've had her out on her ear ages ago if he'd had his way. Liza sighed. It wasn't that easy. You couldn't just sack staff like that these days; especially somebody like Josie May who knew her rights. She'd have them up before an industrial tribunal claiming unfair dismissal—and hefty compensation! —quicker than you could say "Jack Robinson." And besides, there was that business over Ronnie . . . Trust him to come around while Josie was on the desk. How Josie'd found out they'd been married she'd never know! Probably listened at the door the night Ronnie had suddenly turned up whining about his bad luck. So full of self-pity she'd hardly recognised him. The Ronnie she'd known had always been a winner (except as a performer when he'd added a whole new dimension to the meaning of mediocrity!). It had been as an agent and show business manager and promoter that Ronnie had really shone. But, like so many others, he'd always chased after that one elusive thing that was never within the range of his artistic capabilities. A shame. But there you are; that's life!

Liza glanced into the dining-room. Her husband was taking Mrs. (talk of the devil) Charles' order for dinner.

While she waited for her husband to go down to the kitchen where she could talk to him in relative privacy, Liza's thoughts went back to Josie . . .

It wasn't as though the girl had anything on her. She and Ronnie were divorced. All legal and above board. And yet, thought Liza, that was how she felt; as if Josie was just waiting to use what she knew about her and Ronnie against her someday, which was both irritating (because there was no real need for her to feel that way—it was no big deal nowadays to be divorced!), and somehow frightening. She hadn't liked the look of Josie when she had turned up for her first interview for a job; and next time,

Liza vowed to herself, she would have a little more faith in her judgment. In future, anybody—be it male or female—about whom she had those kinds of feelings wouldn't stand a chance. Even if it meant she would end up doing everything in the hotel herself!

CHAPTER 14

"Mrs. Charles! Oh, good," said Liza Murdoch brightly. "I couldn't find you in any of the public rooms and I thought you might've gone out for the evening."

Liza forced herself to smile and tried to sound relaxed and natural. "There's a gentleman waiting to see you in the office; a police inspector from the Sandycombe County Constabulary. I'm sorry I can't find anywhere more private for you to talk, but the lounge is quite full at the moment. And then there's the band." She laughed and frowned at the same time. "You wouldn't be able to hear yourself think! I've got Mr. Murdoch to put up the grille on the reception desk so you won't be disturbed."

Guilt heavily underlined the edginess in Liza's voice and the clairvoyante was aware of it. *Here comes a big chopper to chop off your head,* she thought wryly as she got her room key and then followed Liza up the corridor. No doubt Madame Murdoch would hurry away and fetch her knitting the moment she had delivered her into the hands of the executioner!

Liza introduced the clairvoyante to Detective-Inspector Royal and then withdrew, without a backward glance closing the door of the office quickly and firmly behind her. Then, letting out a small sigh of relief, she put a hand to her right temple and gently massaged it with her fingertips. Her head ached painfully. So did her left hip and knee; a legacy from her circus days. She walked away limping slightly.

Royal was casually dressed in a chunky navy blue fisherman's sweater and a khaki anorak with a small rent in one of its pockets. His black trousers were tucked into the tops of a stout pair of wellingtons. Clean ones; as if he had only just come in off one of the boats. He had an immobile, rather tired expression on his face, and very shrewd brown eyes. Which, the clairvoyante noted, were studying her closely.

Royal transferred his steady gaze from Mrs. Charles' face to her hands. My God! he marvelled to himself. The woman was a walking jewellery store. Between them, she and Liza Murdoch would be worth a small fortune!

He had been standing with his back to the reception desk, leaning against it, when she first came into the office. Then, straightening up, he had gestured to a chair near a small, floor-standing safe. When Mrs. Charles was seated, he drew out the typist's chair and sat down. With his right foot resting on one of the chair's splayed-out aluminium feet, he swivelled slowly from side to side. He spoke quietly with just a trace of tiredness.

"I'm sorry to trouble you, ma'am—" He stared at his hands, which were clasped loosely on his knees, and made slow circling motions with his thumbs. "But I have reason to believe you might be able to help us with our inquiries into the death of Miss Doris Kemp. I understand that you met Miss Kemp at one of the fishermen's cottages up on the cliffs somewhere around lunch-time yesterday."

He stopped twiddling his thumbs and sat perfectly still. Then, looking up quickly as though to make sure that he wasn't talking to himself, and without waiting for her to confirm or deny the allegation, he asked, "How well did you know Miss Kemp?"

"I didn't know her at all," the clairvoyante replied. "We met yesterday for the first time. While I was out walking on the cliffs I noticed a FOR SALE board outside one of the cottages up there, so I went up to a window and looked inside. I wouldn't normally be so impertinent—" she half-smiled "—but the place seemed deserted and I saw no harm in taking a quick look around while I was there. However, as I was looking through the window, a woman—Miss Kemp—came out and spoke to me. She was cleaning the cottage at the time," she explained after a slight pause. "She invited me inside to view the property properly."

"You're interested in buying property in Michaelmas Cove?"

"I always keep an eye out for a good investment; and my accountant assures me that a holiday cottage, one that can be let, is a particularly sound investment these days."

He hunched slightly forward; looked down at his hands again. "How long did you spend going over the property?"

"I must've been there for something like half an hour," she answered, phrasing her reply with a scrupulous regard for the truth. "A bit longer, perhaps. Miss Kemp was a very friendly person and she went out of her way to be helpful. We sat and talked for a while before I left and she told me that the cottage had once belonged to a very close friend of hers who had died in particularly tragic circumstances. She said this was why she was taking care of it."

"Did you leave the cottage together?"

"No. Miss Kemp was still there when I came away. She hadn't finished dusting the sitting-room."

"At what time did you leave?"

"Somewhere around twelve-thirty. I came straight back here to the hotel for lunch."

"Did you see or speak to anyone on the cliffs on your way down?"

"No. I'm afraid I didn't waste a moment about getting back. The weather looked very threatening, as if a storm were brewing. In fact it started to rain before I reached the hotel and I got drenched."

Royal looked up suddenly and said, "You paused at Jupiter's Lookout to speak to someone—a woman—while you were on your way up the cliffs."

"Yes. I said 'good-morning' to a woman sitting on a bench. She didn't reply. Or if she did, I didn't hear her."

Royal hesitated. He had a feeling that some kind of trap had been laid for him but he wasn't sure where. "I understand you and this woman—the one on the bench—know each other."

She widened her eyes. "Is that what she said?"

"It's not true?"

"That all depends on what you mean when you say we know one another. I met her once, very briefly, some years ago; but we were not, as I recall it, formally introduced to one another. I don't even know her name."

"She knows yours," he said.

Mrs. Charles looked at him and waited.

"Does the name Adele Herrmann mean anything to you?"

"It should. It's my name."

"I see." Royal did some more thumb-twiddling. "What about Mrs. E. Charles of The Bungalow, Little Gidding, Nr. Gidding? What's suddenly happened to her?"

"Nothing. Adele Herrmann is my maiden name—the name I use professionally. The other dates back to Charles the Third," she explained with another half-smile. "My third and last husband, that is. One Edwin Charles."

He looked at her.

"Just what line of business are you in, ma'am?" he inquired.

"I'm a consultant specialising in the field of future social and economic trends and their likely effect on the individual," she replied unhesitatingly.

He looked hard at her; wondered what that little lot of gobbledegook meant in simple everyday language. Just about anything; though it sounded suspiciously to him like one of those totally superfluous departments certain branches of the civil service seemed to delight in creating at the taxpayers' expense.

"Have you been here before?" he inquired abruptly.

"To Michaelmas Cove?" Mrs. Charles shook her head. "No; this is my first visit."

He studied her thoughtfully. There was a shrewd intelligence in those dark blue eyes of hers and it bothered him. She hadn't killed Doris Kemp; not if McIntyre were right about the time of death. She was busy eating lunch in The Mermaid's dining-room surrounded by a host of other diners. And yet somehow she was involved in the crime. She had to be. It was no coincidence that she should be out walking on the cliffs yesterday morning while Doris Kemp was cleaning the Mays' cottage, any more than it was a coincidence that the initials of her maiden name should later be discovered near Doris Kemp's body. One went with the other. Any fool could see that . . . But *who* left her initials there? Doris Kemp? (In which case this rather self-assured, enigmatic woman lied about not knowing the dead woman prior to her stopping at the Mays' cottage yesterday.) Or the witness who came forward with information about Adele Herrmann? Two visitors to Michaelmas Cove who didn't want to tell the police what they were really doing there. They had used different tricks to dodge the issue. In response to the questions that Spence had put to the other witness which she had not wished to answer (like the one about her reason for being in Michaelmas Cove yesterday), she had whirled about like a dervish (Spence had claimed), and had quoted long passages of "witch-talk" from what Spence thought might have been Shakespeare. And as for Mrs. E. for Edwin Charles, thought Royal . . . She had skilfully taken everything he had said to her and turned it round for her own purpose. She was no more interested in buying property in Michaelmas Cove than he was. She went up the cliffs yesterday morning to meet Doris Kemp: he'd bet his bottom dollar on it. The question was *why?*

Royal rose; thanked Mrs. Charles for her time; asked how long she intended to remain in Michaelmas Cove; and then bade her a good-evening.

He was still in the office when Liza Murdoch returned several minutes after the clairvoyante had left. She gave a start when she saw him. "Oh," she exclaimed. "I'm terribly sorry. I saw Mrs. Charles in the hall and I naturally thought you'd gone."

"Just leaving," he said and started for the door. "Good-night, Mrs. Murdoch. Thank you for the use of the office."

"Inspector . . ."

He paused and turned back to her. She was standing quite still with a transfixed expression on her immaculately made-up face. She reminded him of a tall, statuesque showgirl from a Paris night-club revue. It didn't even take much imagination to picture her in masses of ostrich feathers and not much else.

"Yes, Mrs. Murdoch?"

She moved slightly and the showgirl illusion was shattered. She clasped her hands in front of her and looked down at them. "I wonder if I might have a private word with you? In absolute confidence, I mean. You see . . ." She looked up at him; smiled self-consciously. "This is very embarrassing for me, Inspector. I wouldn't want my husband to know I've spoken to you about this, but I think it would be wrong of me not to say something." She walked up to the reception desk and looked through the black wrought-iron grille. Then, turning to face him, she said, "Josie May has been talking to some of the other members of the staff—"

"About your ex-husband?"

She was mildly taken aback by his directness. Then, with a resigned gesture: "About Ronnie and Dee. Deanna Bastian. Josie's been hinting that Dee was pregnant by Ronnie and I just wanted you to know that it isn't true. It can't be; it simply isn't possible. Ronnie had a vasectomy. Long before he married me. During our marriage he underwent further surgery to have the operation reversed, but it was a failure. His first wife—the woman to whom he was married before he married me—suffered from some rare, inevitably fatal hereditary disease which would've been passed on to any children of hers and that was why she couldn't—or rather, wouldn't—have any, and why Ronnie agreed to the vasectomy. I'm telling you all this for Ronnie's sake. He won't discuss the vasectomy with anyone. He didn't mind it so much while he thought it could be reversed. But afterwards; after the doctors told him there was no hope—" She turned away; looked through the grille for a moment, then placed her hands flat on the counter and gazed at their long scarlet nails. "Well, it was a major factor contributing to the breakdown of our marriage—that and the fact that our separate show business careers kept us apart for lengthy periods of time. He can't bear anyone knowing—" She turned back suddenly and looked at him. "What I'm really trying to say is this . . . If rumours about Ronnie and Dee and her being pregnant begin to spread and you—the police —want to talk to him about it, he'll never admit to not being able to father a child. He'd die first . . ."

"Deanna wasn't pregnant, Mrs. Murdoch," said Royal. She wasn't virgo intacta either; but that, he thought, while it was not entirely irrelevant, was hardly any of Liza Murdoch's business. "But thank you for being so frank with me."

"I'm glad," she said. "About Dee; that what Josie's been saying isn't true." She hesitated; seemed undecided, as if there were something else she wanted to say. Or there was something she expected him to say.

"I had to say something about Ronnie," she said after a moment. "I was only a bit of a girl; just another acrobatic dancer going nowhere special until he took me under his wing and made a big international star out of me. I feel I owe him."

But not as much as you feel you owe yourself to keep him out of this mess, thought Royal cynically. If Deanna Bastian had been pregnant and an intimate relationship between her and this Ronnie were subsequently established, then regardless of whether or not he was capable of fathering a child, Liza Murdoch's private business would've suddenly gone public. Very public. And that would be intolerable for someone like her who liked to think of herself as being a cut above the local peasantry. That was the impression she gave him, anyway. Big international star indeed! He'd never heard of her. Other than from her own lips, that is!

As he left The Mermaid a minute or two later, he heavily underscored the mental note he had made earlier never to get on the wrong side of Josie May. She would get worse as she grew older. A sobering thought. Spence had spoken to Penny Reynolds again late that afternoon and she had told him what had taken place at her home on Sunday night when Josie May had brought her ouija board round and suggested they try it out. Penny claimed that Deanna had been very upset and scared, both while they were using the ouija board and afterwards. Mainly, Penny thought, because of a near-fatal accident Deanna had once had in a swimming-pool. The ouija board's message for Deanna that night had apparently been concerned with water and a fatality. And then the next morning at work, she had been worried and depressed and abnormally absent-minded. Mrs. Bastian had known nothing about Josie May's ouija board until Spence had mentioned it to her. It also came out during the course of the sergeant's conversation with Mrs. Bastian that

Deanna sometimes suffered from severe premenstrual tension (and she was coming up to her period when she died, Mrs. Bastian told Spence) which made her over-anxious and depressed. Easily upset. Mrs. Bastian had seemed shocked by the suggestion that Deanna might've been suicidal at these times; but McIntyre, when Royal had raised the matter with him, had said he knew of a number of instances where young women suffering from a severe form of P.M.T. regularly made attempts on their lives at this time each month if they were not receiving proper medical treatment for the condition, or the treatment was suspended for a time. Deanna had not consulted a doctor about her anxiety and depression. The Bastians were Christian Scientists and did not approve of doctors or drug-taking for any reason.

Sighing, Royal opened the door of his car, then paused momentarily and looked back at the hotel. Music wafted across the forecourt from the lounge, the windows of which were lined with a spasmodically animated single row of identically permed and set grey-haired heads. Two elderly women were dancing with one another. They flitted across one of the windows and vanished. He wondered that they could be bothered.

CHAPTER 15

Mrs. Charles double-locked the door of her room, turned and paused. It was back again; that strong sense of foreboding. A feeling of being surrounded by ill will and hostility.

Frowning, she crossed thoughtfully to the window and stood looking out at the floodlit swimming-pool. The dance music being played in the lounge filtered softly through the walls, but she didn't hear it. She was thinking about Peggy May's letter; the references she had made in it to the hermit.

The Hermit: the possessor of a secret. A secret that may not necessarily ever be revealed . . .

The clairvoyante concentrated her thoughts on this, the ninth card in the Major Arcana of the Tarot, and the key card in Peggy May's reading.

It was the one thing she must never lose sight of, Mrs. Charles reminded herself. It was the hermit and the hermit alone who had sealed Peggy's fate. The hermit and his secret were there first. Peggy came after the fact.

The clairvoyante went back carefully over her conversation with Doris Kemp. The key to the hermit's secret was definitely contained somewhere within its framework. Doris Kemp had said something to her which had come so dangerously close to revealing his secret that she had become a serious threat to someone. But *what?* What had Doris said to her that had so badly alarmed the person whom the clairvoyante believed to have been watching and listening beyond the door of the cottage yesterday lunchtime that Doris' life had immediately become forfeit?

Two things, Mrs. Charles decided at length. The first that Doris had admitted to not liking Mary Farrow. This, when the clairvoyante analysed their conversation, stood out like a beacon.

Doris had denied knowing the reason for her dislike of the woman (and in all probability she had been quite sincere in this); but nevertheless her subconscious knew what had caused her to feel that way about her. The clairvoyante was as sure of this now as when actually talking to Doris. And the second (and perhaps more important of the two possible motives for her murder) . . . Doris had seen Peggy's mysterious gentleman caller and had actually discussed him with her friend.

Doris had implied that he was a stranger to the village. But maybe he was nothing of the sort. She had admitted to some pretence with Peggy when she had tried to find out what had been going on between her friend and this man; and very possibly, Doris had been similarly deceitful yesterday. Loyalty to her dead friend and to her own kind—a villager like herself—might have held her back from disclosing the man's true identity to an outsider. Doris had genuinely wanted to help her (there was no doubt in the clairvoyante's mind about that); but there might have been limits to how far she had been prepared to go with that help. Michaelmas Cove's past links with smuggling and the stranger with a scarred face could have been convenient fictions used by her to conceal the real identity of Peggy's lover. What then, in those circumstances, was the motive for Doris' murder? the clairvoyante asked herself. Doris hadn't disclosed the man's identity to her; obviously hadn't shown any sign in the past of being a threat to him because of what she knew by spreading gossip around the village. Doris wasn't the gossipy type. And that person, if he were someone local, would've known it; known that she was a good and loyal friend and that it was highly unlikely that he would ever have any real cause to fear her. And yet that was what Doris' murder had almost certainly been; an act of very real fear. Somebody—maybe more than one person—was terribly afraid that she (Adele Herrmann, that is) was going to discover the hermit's secret. But why leave her initials in the dirt near Doris' body? More to the point, *who* left them there? Definitely someone who knew Adele Herrmann. Somebody from the pre-Charles the Third period of her life . . .

Or Doris Kemp herself.

The clairvoyante shaded her eyes with her hand; waited for her thoughts to clear.

She had told Courtney Harrington that Doris Kemp knew her maiden name. But now that she thought about it, Doris never referred to her by name at the cottage. Not once. ". . . *the clairvoyante . . . the one Peggy wrote to* . . ." That was how Doris had identified her.

But this wasn't to say that Peggy hadn't mentioned the name Adele Herrmann to her.

The clairvoyante frowned. If Doris had known her name, and it was she who had scratched her initials in the dirt, then that made it something personal between her, Adele Herrmann, and Doris. There was no mystery for the police to solve. Doris had been trying to tell *her* something. Not them.

Had she remembered what she had forgotten?

The clairvoyante dropped her hand from her face and her eyes opened wide.

Mary Farrow. It *had* to be her. Something there; something Doris had known about her which somebody wanted well and truly forgotten.

Mrs. Charles looked quickly at the time. No, it was too late now. It would have to wait until morning. And in the meanwhile she would just have to be patient and hope that Courtney Harrington would know somebody who could help her.

The clairvoyante took one last look at the swimming-pool and then closed the curtains.

The swami sighed and shook his head regretfully as Mrs. Charles explained her quest.

It was early the following morning and the old man looked tired and rumpled, as if a disturbed night had left him apathetic and inert.

"I can't help you there, 'Del," he said. "I haven't lived here long enough to know that sort of thing. One hears a certain amount of gossip, of course; but if, as you've just said, Mary Farrow left Michaelmas Cove and went into domestic service, then that period of her life—what happened to her during those years—

has probably never gone into the local rumour mill. And in any event, I'm not really one of them, you know; a local born and bred. There are some things I'd never get to hear. What you need is someone who worked on—what was it, the Easterbrook estate, did you say?—while she was employed there."

The clairvoyante widened her eyes at him, but he shook his head. They lapsed into a dejected silence.

"If," said the swami at length, "you're sure that Doris Kemp knew something about Mary Farrow which wasn't common knowledge, then it occurs to me that the chances are her sister would more than likely know what it was too."

"Sister? Doris Kemp had a sister?"

"Yes; Phyllis—Mrs. Trout. Good few years older than Doris, I believe. She lives over in Sandycombe. She and her family moved there after the old doctor—Dr. Kemp, her father—died. She used to all but run his practice for him near the end. The old boy was as near as dammit blind and deaf as a post, and Phyllis—who I understand had had some nursing training with the Red Cross during the last war—had to be around constantly to make sure that he didn't kill anybody off by writing out a wrong prescription or something of the kind. He should've been pensioned off, but you know how it is. If they'd brought in somebody new, nobody in the village would've gone to him. Not while there was still breath left in the old boy."

Mrs. Charles nodded. Then, after a brief pause, she said, "It would seem, then, that this Mrs. Trout is my only hope."

"It looks a bit like it," he agreed.

Mrs. Charles rose, then frowned and said, "By the way, I've been thinking about Fr. Thomas' accident up on the cliffs. I don't suppose you'd remember exactly when it happened?"

"Yes, as a matter of fact I do remember. A lot of people, including myself, blamed it—his distress—for his fall. He'd been drinking, of course: there's no point—" he shrugged "—in anybody denying that; but it was the night Albert May died."

It was shortly before 3:30 P.M., in a fine, almost tropical drizzle of rain, that the clairvoyante arrived at the address in Sandycombe which Courtney Harrington had looked up for her that morning.

Phyllis Trout answered the door. She strongly resembled her late sister, except in build. Doris had been tall and slightly built, whereas her older sister had a well-rounded, matronly figure over a more solid bone structure.

The two women exchanged polite greetings and then Mrs. Charles said, "I'm sorry to trouble you, Mrs. Trout. I am Edwina Charles. The police might possibly have mentioned my name to you in connection with your sister Doris."

"Edwina Charles?" murmured the other woman. The puzzled expression on her face suddenly lifted. "Oh yes, I remember now . . . Aren't you the lady who's interested in buying some property in Michaelmas Cove? Inspector Royal called round this morning and mentioned something about it."

Nothing registered on Mrs. Charles' face, or in her eyes, but she was taking careful stock of Phyllis Trout. There was kindness and intelligence in her soft grey eyes. A certain shrewdness. She was a woman whom Mrs. Charles felt she could trust. Up to a point . . .

"That was the story I gave to the police," the clairvoyante admitted. "But it wasn't the real reason why I went up to the cottage where your sister was working on Tuesday morning. I went there because it belonged to someone I used to know; someone I hadn't seen in twenty-five years. Peggy May—Baldwin, as I knew her."

There was an odd expression on Phyllis Trout's face; something covert about the look in her eyes. Abruptly, she turned aside from the door and said, "I think perhaps you'd better come inside."

They went through to a neat, plainly furnished living-room and sat down.

The clairvoyante looked deep into the other woman's eyes. There had been a change; a very slight change, but a change none the less. Phyllis Trout had all her defences up. She was very much on her guard and made no attempt to speak, waiting watchfully in the lengthening silence for her visitor to explain herself.

Mrs. Charles was in no hurry. After a very long moment, she said quietly, "You didn't like Peggy May, did you? In fact, I think you hated her. Quite passionately, I shouldn't wonder."

Phyllis Trout looked startled: blinked once, twice, then three times in rapid succession. She opened her mouth to deny what the clairvoyante had said, but closed it again without uttering a sound. After a short pause, she made another false start; and then, finally, she said, "How did you know? Did Doris tell you this?"

The clairvoyante shook her head. "No, Mrs. Trout. It's in your eyes. You strongly disapproved of their friendship."

As Phyllis Trout looked at her, the caution in her eyes melted slowly away. She sighed. "Do you believe that there are some people in this world whose influence, not by their actual exertion of that influence, quite unwittingly, is for bad, while the influence of others is likewise for good?"

"I do indeed. Most strongly," said the clairvoyante.

Phyllis Trout nodded her head slowly. "Peggy May was a bad influence—a bad influence without ever having made that her real intention. Doris was fifteen years younger than I am which meant that I had as much to do with her upbringing as our parents did. And if ever she was in any trouble, you could be sure that at the bottom of it you would find Peggy Baldwin. Trivial little things, mostly. Silly, brainless, idiotical things—" she frowned "—that Doris, if it hadn't been for Peggy's influence, would've had more sense than to have got herself involved in. Larking about with boys. Getting herself a bad name."

"The Peggy I recall," said the clairvoyante, "was a most attractive young woman who, I'm sure, would've had a great many male admirers."

"That she most certainly did!" said Phyllis Trout emphatically. "A shortage of boy-friends was one problem Peggy Baldwin never had to cope with. She could've had her pick of any of the village boys. Sir Percival Easterbrook's son was even smitten with her and asked her to marry him. At least, that was the rumour. But she had her head up in the clouds about becoming a dancer, and off she went. Left all the boys high and dry, including Albert—the man she eventually married and to whom she was practically engaged. And Doris . . ." Phyllis Trout's tone became bitter. "Once Peggy took off, nobody gave Doris a second glance. It was a bad time for her . . . adjusting to the change in her life that not having Peggy Baldwin around had made. And, of course, Doris never married. If any of the young men in the village did bother to call on her after Peggy went, it was only to ask after her, Peggy. Had Doris heard from her; when was Peggy coming home . . . ?" She sighed. "What a waste; what a terrible waste. Doris was worth ten of her. And now nobody will ever know it. Doris is dead. Murdered. Just when it'd seemed to me that she was beginning to settle down. At last, I thought, she was going to start making some sense of her life. There was still time. She was only forty-eight; not unattractive. If anyone should've been murdered," she said vehemently, "it was Peggy. Years ago."

"Peggy *was* murdered, Mrs. Trout."

Phyllis Trout stared at the clairvoyante. "What d'you mean? Peggy committed suicide. After her husband died."

The clairvoyante was shaking her head. "No, Mrs. Trout. Peggy May was murdered. By the same person, I believe, who murdered your sister."

CHAPTER 16

"I—" Several times Phyllis Trout's mouth opened and closed like that of a tropical fish with its face pressed up against the side of its glass tank. "How—?" She paused, frowned, then tried again: "What makes you say that?"

"I am a clairvoyante, Mrs. Trout. Twenty-five years ago, Peggy May—Baldwin as she was then—asked me to read the cards, the Tarot, for her. It was in her reading that sooner or later she would be murdered."

Phyllis Trout laughed. "You'll forgive me, but you don't seriously expect me to believe that, do you?"

"I would like you to try," said the clairvoyante quietly. "Particularly as it's the truth."

Phyllis Trout looked at her; wondered why this woman should suddenly make her feel so doubtful about something which she had never before queried. "All right," she said hesitantly. "Let's suppose, just for the moment, that I do believe you. Did she, Peggy, know this . . . that she was going to be murdered one day?"

"No. I decided not to tell her. I chose instead to give her a warning which, properly interpreted (something Peggy could've done for herself when a certain sequence of events came to pass), would've saved her from what I believe was her own self-destruction, even though the actual physical act of taking her life was perpetrated by another's hand."

"What was your warning; the one you gave her?" asked Phyllis Trout cautiously.

"I didn't elaborate . . ." The clairvoyante paused and considered carefully what she should say next. She decided not to be too explicit and to deviate, as others had before her, slightly from the truth. "Very broadly speaking," she then went on, "I simply advised Peggy to beware of the hermit—" she hesitated briefly "—and of the girl who is clairvoyant. That was enough to save Peggy from herself."

"The girl who is clairvoyant?" Phyllis mouthed the words in a bewildered whisper. *"Pearl Farrow?* Is that who you mean?"

The clairvoyante avoided a direct answer. "Your sister told me that she (Doris) didn't like Mary Farrow. Why was that, Mrs. Trout? What reason did your sister have for disliking Mary Farrow?"

There was a genuinely surprised look in Phyllis Trout's eyes. She shook her head. "I don't know— Doris never said anything like that to me. I didn't think they knew one another all that well. Mary is a few years older than Doris. She's not as old as I am, but there was enough of an age gap between the two of them, I would've thought, to have kept them fairly well apart while they were growing up. Didn't Doris give you a reason?"

"No. It was only something she herself realised while she was talking to me about her. Even she didn't know why she disliked her. Something happened between them, Mrs. Trout; something which I believe your sister deliberately made herself forget."

Phyllis Trout was shaking her head slowly. "Nothing that I can recall." She frowned. "Are you *sure* about this?"

"Quite sure. Something definitely happened, Mrs. Trout . . . In Michaelmas Cove; I think somewhere about the time—" the clairvoyante's eyes widened questioningly "—a short while afterwards, perhaps?—that Peggy left the village. If not something directly concerning your sister and Mary Farrow, then indirectly through some third person."

Phyllis Trout looked at Mrs. Charles for a very long moment without saying anything. Then, with downcast eyes, she said, "I'm sorry: I can't help you there."

The clairvoyante nodded. "I see—" She got to her feet. "I think I understand," she said.

Phyllis Trout looked up at her quickly. "But you *don't* understand. You can't . . ."

The clairvoyante smiled coldly. "I really do understand, Mrs.

Trout. Perfectly. Many times over the years I, as a clairvoyante, have found myself placed in a similar position of absolute trust where to break a confidence would be as morally wrong—sinful, if you like—as to reveal the secrets of the confessional. I am aware that you worked closely with your father, the village doctor, and I respect the confidence and the trust that he and his patients placed in you."

A strange expression crossed the other woman's face. Relief, thought the clairvoyante, puzzled. So the secret didn't lie there, within the framework of a doctor/patient relationship. Admittedly, she had been stabbing wildly in the dark, but all the same, it wasn't often that her natural instinct for this kind of thing left her so wide of the mark.

Phyllis Trout hesitated. Then, carefully: "There's one thing I can tell you without breaking anyone's confidence. After she retired, Sir Percival Easterbrook's old cook—a Mrs. Sowerby—went to live in the village (Michaelmas Cove) and signed on with my father. As one of his patients, I mean. This was shortly before my father died; and Mrs. Sowerby has herself since passed on . . . quite some while ago now, in fact—"

"Yes?" prompted Mrs. Charles when the narrative suddenly came to a full stop.

"Well, it was something she said to me; just conversationally, you understand, while she was sitting in the waiting-room one day shortly before going in to see my father. She asked me about the young parlourmaid who came from Michaelmas Cove—the one who was up on the Easterbrook estate. 'Her young man made a decent woman of her, I suppose,' she said to me. 'A fine old scandal that was, I must say.'" Phyllis Trout hesitated, then looked down at her hands, moistened her lips and added, "'Poor girl. A right fool he made of her.'"

"Mary Farrow?"

Phyllis Trout's quick nod was only barely discernible.

"'Poor girl' . . . Are those your words? Or were you quoting the Easterbrooks' cook?"

"Her words," she said abruptly.

"What did you say in reply?"

Phyllis Trout made a dismissive gesture with her hand. She didn't look up. "This was years ago. I don't remember now. I think I said she'd married young Jimmy Farrow. Yes," she said uneasily. "That was it; I said she'd got married."

"To the farm labourer—the man who later lost his life in a wheat silo?"

"Yes," said Phyllis Trout, again plainly relieved about something.

The clairvoyante regarded her contemplatively. "Mary Farrow was pregnant at the time of her marriage, but her husband wasn't the father of her unborn child."

The other woman avoided her eyes. "I can't answer that question. If it is a question. You must draw your own conclusions."

"When in relation to her leaving the village did this marriage take place?"

Phyllis Trout shook her head; kept her eyes down. "I'm not sure. It was a long while ago."

"Seventeen years ago?" asked the clairvoyante thoughtfully. "Or was it a longer period of time than that; something more like twenty-five years ago?"

"Probably somewhere nearer to that, twenty-five years. A bit longer, perhaps," Phyllis Trout added evasively.

"Somewhere around the time that Peggy Baldwin left the village?" suggested Mrs. Charles. "What would that have been? Something like twenty-seven years ago?"

"It could've been; I don't remember." Phyllis Trout paused. Then, frowning, she said, "There's no reason why I should remember. Things like that—" Her voice tailed off.

"Things like what, Mrs. Trout?" asked the clairvoyante quietly. "Girls getting themselves into trouble and having to get married; is that what you were about to say?"

Phyllis Trout didn't answer right away. She seemed to be debating something with herself.

"It was what I was going to say," she then went on to admit, "but it wouldn't have been true. Not in Mary Farrow's case." A passionate light showed in her eyes, then suddenly it died and with it the urge to carry on and say something else.

"What do you mean?" asked Mrs. Charles, frowning.

The other woman's lips set in a firm, straight line. Her expression hardened. She looked at Mrs. Charles for a moment, then down at her hands again. "I can't say any more. I've already said more than I should've. I don't know why I've told you this much. You could never understand. You're an outsider. There are things . . . sad, tragic, sometimes quite incredibly cruel and horrid things that happen in small places like Michaelmas Cove and they can never be talked about . . . *never!*" she repeated emphatically.

Mrs. Charles eyed her thoughtfully. "And that tragedy—whatever it was—which befell Mary Farrow all those years ago then touched Peggy May and finally your sister. And goodness knows how many other people before somebody finds the courage to stand up and talk about it."

"I can't—" said Phyllis Trout, a note of pleading in her voice. "It's not for me to say. You don't understand."

"So you've said." The clairvoyante spoke coldly. "Very well, then: can you tell me what became of the child?"

"The child?" Phyllis Trout looked up at her blankly.

"The child of the tragedy who would, *must* be, if he or she is still alive, somewhere in its middle to late twenties. Pearl Farrow is only a teenager. Seventeen, I've been told." The clairvoyante paused and considered the other woman speculatively. "The child died?"

"I can't answer that. It would be a breach of the trust my father's patients placed in him as their family doctor and friend."

"Yes, of course. Please forgive my impertinence."

Phyllis Trout looked at the clairvoyante; frowned. *"Why?"* she said angrily. "Why have you come here? What good can possibly come of raking up all these old tragedies? They're best forgotten."

"I couldn't agree more."

"Then why don't you go back to wherever it is that you've come from and let things be?"

"I can't, Mrs. Trout. There's a great deal more at stake here than the preservation of one or two people's guilty consciences—"

The front doorbell rang. Phyllis Trout jumped up nervously from the sofa and went to the window; peered out at the frail, stooped man dressed in black waiting at the door. "I'm sorry," she said quickly, turning back to Mrs. Charles. "I'll have to ask you to leave now. It's Fr. Thomas—" She hesitated. Then, abruptly: "You know, the funeral arrangements. For Doris."

The clairvoyante met her gaze steadily. They were not Catholics: Doris had said so herself. And there would be no funeral arrangements to be seen to for some while yet; possibly not until after the inquest.

"I'm sorry to have taken up so much of your time," she said. "You've been most kind and considerate. Thank you for seeing me."

At the door, Mrs. Charles said good-afternoon to the priest who waited beyond, nervously twisting his black Homburg hat in his hands; then she thanked Phyllis Trout again and stepped out onto the porch.

Her eyes flicked only very briefly over the white-haired, troubled-looking priest, but it was enough to tell her what she wanted to know. Fr. Michael Thomas' hell-raising days were over for good. He looked an old man and yet as a boyhood chum of Albert May's, he was more than likely still only in his fifties. Other tell-tale signs of alcoholism were there too. The enlarged nose with its deep purple bloom; the angry red network of broken facial veins; blurred irises. But Fr. Thomas was labouring out the remainder of his years under some other greater, more terrible burden. And whatever that burden was, if he didn't (and he probably couldn't) relieve himself of it very soon or have someone carry out that onerous task for him, it would destroy him; poison him as surely and fatally as the alcohol would before very long. He was a wretched man, piteously so. Haunted, yes; but haunted by what? mused the clairvoyante as she started back to Michaelmas Cove. The burden of what and whose sin did Fr. Michael Thomas carry around with him?

The questions kept going round and round inside her head.

Was Ida Claythorpe right about the old man?

Did somebody really try to kill him the night his friend, Albert May, died?

Just how much store should she place in the old lady's intuitiveness; her powers of perception? She had spoken with great feeling and compassion for Pearl Farrow and for her own mentally retarded brother. Mrs. Charles recalled the softness which had come into Mrs. Claythorpe's eyes, the gentleness of her voice when she had spoken of him; his childishly youthful appearance at the time of his death, notwithstanding his advanced years—

A sudden jolt went through the clairvoyante which left her momentarily shaken.

Pearl Farrow . . . There was no other child; there never had been! Pearl was the child, the illegitimate child to whom the innocent farm labourer, James Farrow, had given his name. Pearl was anything up to ten years older than her mother had let on to the people of Michaelmas Cove. Dr. Kemp and his daughter Phyllis had known the truth. A doctor wouldn't have been deceived by Mary Farrow's claim that her daughter was younger than she really was; and the Farrows had almost certainly been Dr. Kemp's patients . . .

Was this what Doris had remembered after leaving the cottage?

Mrs. Charles frowned. But surely Doris would hardly be likely to forget, or feel the need to block out, something like that?

No, there had to be something else.

But what?

CHAPTER 17

The clairvoyante knew long before she reached her brother that he had some news for her. He was skipping up and down on the spot outside the coach station like a child, beaming all over his face.

"Guess what, 'Del," he greeted her, his dark eyes shining with the excitement he had been obliged to suppress throughout his long journey down to the West Country. "Harry's driving over to Michaelmas Cove after lunch tomorrow to fetch us. He's entered the soap-box derby and we're going to watch him race."

"In his coffin, no doubt," said Mrs. Charles in a dry aside, relieving her brother of his lighter hand luggage. And he had an unusual amount of it considering that he was staying for only a week-end. "Really, Cyril," she went on reprovingly. "You might have discussed it with me first before making any definite arrangements with your friend."

He looked at her slyly. "Harry used to live in Michaelmas Cove. He was born there. And what's more, there was some trouble between him and the local people a few years back over one of his publicity stunts that went wrong. He was supposed to escape from a blazing pile of packing crates down on the beach near the quay; only the wind changed."

"And?" said Mrs. Charles when he paused.

"The quay caught on fire, didn't it?" Implicit in Cyril's tone was his assumption that his sister would have deduced as much for herself. There were some things, especially where his friend Harry was concerned, which went without saying.

Cyril's eyebrows shot up expressively. "Half the fishing fleet went up in smoke. The villagers as good as ran Harry out of Michaelmas Cove." Cyril paused and gave his sister a sidelong look. "There's a lot of bad feeling in him about that place. Not too much loyalty, I'd say. If I were asked, that is," he added airily. "He got quite hostile about it when I spoke to him on the phone yesterday afternoon. You never know what a fellow like that might be likely to tell a person."

Mrs. Charles gave her brother a thoughtful look. "Beneath that benign, somewhat scatty exterior you present to the outside world, Cyril," she observed at length, "lies the complicated workings of a very devious, thoroughly crafty mind."

"Yes," he said simply.

Immediately after lunch, the clairvoyante and her brother took a stroll along Michaelmas Cove's long sandy beach.

The day was sunny and warm and they walked for a time in companionable silence, neither one of them showing any inclination for conversation until the sweeping curve of the deep, crescent-shaped cove brought them to a rocky outcrop which barred their way and they were obliged to turn and retrace their steps.

As they started back, Mrs. Charles said, "Now, let's get down to business, shall we? I daresay I won't get much sense out of you once your friend Harry turns up tomorrow; so I should appreciate it if you'd give me your undivided attention and concentrate your mind, if only for five minutes, on our real reason for being in Michaelmas Cove."

"Yes, 'Del," he said dutifully. "I'm concentrating."

"Good," she said, eyeing him doubtfully.

"Tell me everything you know or have discovered about Tweedledee."

"But I've told you all I know about her," he protested, his thoughts already straying to the visit to Sandycombe planned for the following day.

"Then tell me again," she said insistently.

He sighed. "Her name is Rita Jones and she used to work for Bridger."

"There seemed to be a lot more to it than that the first time round," she said when he paused.

There was a long silence.

Mrs. Charles waited patiently.

"Bridger got her work for a time. This was after he gave up the concert party to concentrate on his show business agency."

A further silence; this one longer again. Then Cyril said, "It's a funny thing . . . You remember how I said I thought Peggy Baldwin tried to commit suicide over some fellow—"

"You also said you thought it could've been one of the girls in the dancing troupe," his sister reminded him. "And that if it were Peggy, it might've been because of her weight problem."

He nodded and lapsed into a dreamy silence.

"It was," he said after a while.

"It was what?"

"Her. Peggy Baldwin. And it was over a fellow. A married man. And not just any married man."

Mrs. Charles halted and looked searchingly at her brother. He didn't notice and continued on alone along the beach.

The clairvoyante hastened to catch up with him. "Bridger?" she asked a little breathlessly.

"I just said so, didn't I?" he responded, completely unaware that no one had been walking beside him for the past minute or so.

"So that was why he was always hovering about her," she remarked absently.

Cyril said, "I thought it was because she ate too much and he thought she'd end up too fat for a dancer."

"He was skulking in the background while I was reading the cards for her that night," said the clairvoyante. She eyed her brother curiously. "Who told you all of this?"

"The same fellow who told me about Rita Jones and Bridger. This chap and Bridger used to be mates back in Bridger's concert party days. He still sees Bridger occasionally when Bridger's up his way."

"I wish you'd mentioned this to me over the phone the other night," she said, frowning at him.

"I forgot," he said simply. "You know what I am, 'Del."

She sighed. "Never mind. It probably wouldn't have made any difference."

"What sort of difference could it have made?"

"If I'd known about this before, I could've asked the sister of Peggy's best friend Doris—the 'Dorrie' Peggy mentioned in her letter to me—if she knew anything about Peggy's affair with Bridger."

"Why not ask Peggy's friend; this Dorrie?"

"I can't now, Cyril. It's too late for that. She's dead. She was murdered several days ago. Her body was found on the cliffs shortly after I'd been talking to her up there about Peggy." Mrs. Charles hesitated; frowned. "I recall, though, that Doris said that while Peggy never made any direct reference to it in any of her letters home, she (Doris) felt that there was a man in Peggy's life . . . someone other than Albert, the boy she'd left behind."

"The fellow she eventually married?"

Mrs. Charles nodded. "Anything else you've forgotten to tell me?"

"About Bridger and Peggy Baldwin? No, I don't think so." Cyril was silent for a moment. Then: "Peggy swallowed all the aspirin after Bridger confessed to her that he was married and couldn't marry her."

"I wonder how long that was—the suicide attempt, I mean—before I read the cards for her?"

"My memory's not too good, 'Del—you know that; but my impression is that it wasn't all that long before that night. Everyone was still keeping an eye on her to make sure she didn't have another go at the aspirin bottle." He narrowed his eyes reflectively. "I'm not a hundred per cent sure about this, but I've an idea they were so worried about her that one of the girls who was looking after her even took it on herself to write home and tell Peggy's family what had happened. The girls used to talk to me and tell me all their troubles, but I wasn't always listening. Not properly. You know how it is with me," he said with a shrug.

"That could fit," his sister said musingly. "What you just said about one of the girls writing to Peggy's family. It could possibly account for Albert May's sudden appearance that night. Peggy's family might've gone to him and told him what had been going on between her and Bridger, and so he came after her to fetch. her back home."

"He was very fond of her."

"Who? Albert May?"

"No, Bridger. The fellow I spoke to told me it was more than just a passing affair as far as Bridger was concerned. Bridger hoped Peggy would accept the situation as it was."

"What d'you mean?" His sister frowned at him. "Accept that he was a married man and settle for the role of mistress instead of wife?"

Cyril shrugged and left her to draw her own conclusions.

"But instead," she went on slowly, "she ran off back home with Albert, her childhood sweetheart."

"Probably did it to spite him . . . Bridger." Cyril paused and considered the possibility. Then: "I doubt that it would've bothered him too much, though. Somebody would've stepped into her shoes before long. He was a real ladies' man, you know. I'm surprised you don't remember more about him."

Mrs. Charles shot her brother a quick look. "I'm not sure I know what you mean by that remark, Cyril. I used to see him occasionally on the pier as he was making his way down to the theatre and I remember that he was tall; popular, as you've said, with the girls. And he had a very nice voice; I recall thinking that when he came up and spoke to Peggy that night at the party. But aside from that the man made little or no impression on me at all. I had other fish to fry."

Cyril thrust his hands into the pockets of his trousers and jingled some loose coins. "He was a strange sort of cove; never really loved and left any of his old girl-friends. Even after he dropped the agency and became a sales rep, he still kept in touch with his girls; or they kept in touch with him. The ones who used to work for him, I mean. This chap I was talking to told me Bridger still gives them advice about their careers; and he'll even use his old show business contacts to get them work if they're really down on their luck."

Cyril paused and looked at his sister; wondered why she was staring at him.

"Have I said something wrong?" he asked.

"Bridger is a sales rep now?"

"That's right. For a chocolate firm, I think. He spends nearly all his time on the road."

Mrs. Charles continued to stare at her brother. "Why didn't you tell me this before?" she demanded.

"I did," he said imperturbably. "You couldn't have been listening. It's important, is it?"

"If Bridger's the man who met Peggy secretly in the caves on the fourteenth of each month," she replied thoughtfully.

"You think they picked up again from where they'd left off all those years ago?"

"You said Bridger was very fond of her," she reminded him, a puzzled expression in her eyes. And Albert May was dying; a bedridden invalid . . . She sighed to herself. It didn't add up. There was one man too many. If Bridger was Peggy's secret lover, who was the scar-faced man Doris met up with on the cliffs the night Albert May died?

"Did your friend say what area Bridger covered?" she inquired. "Would Michaelmas Cove be on his patch, I wonder?"

"I never bothered to ask," said Cyril. "You didn't tell me you were gunning for Bridger too. It was Rita Jones I was supposed to inquire about."

Brother and sister remained silent for quite some time, their thoughts miles apart. Then, with typical abruptness, Cyril's mind was catapulted back onto the subject under discussion.

"I don't get it," he said. "How does Bridger fit in with the reading you did for Peggy and the warning you gave her about the hermit and the girl who is clairvoyant?"

Mrs. Charles widened her eyes at him. "Good heavens, Cyril: I should've thought that would've been patently obvious to you. You yourself remarked how Bridger hovered about her that night. He overheard every word we said . . ."

CHAPTER 18

Harry Brent was a small man, middle-aged, unnervingly wall-eyed behind prism-lensed spectacles, and had thick platinum blond hair which he bleached and tinted himself.

He was wearing a bottle-green velvet suit with a much paler green polka dot shirt and a necktie of thin black cord secured at the throat with a small gold skull ring. Genuine snakeskin cowboy boots with exaggerated high heels elevated him to a height of five feet five inches.

But for the lack of at least one ear-ring and some bizarre face make-up, he could have been the lead singer with a pop group, thought the clairvoyante as she shook his limp, rather clammy hand.

The shiny black limousine in which she and her brother travelled to Sandycombe early the following afternoon was brand new and looked suspiciously like a mourner's motor car. Harry did not mention what he was currently doing for a living, but there was something about the very formal manner in which he sat at the wheel of the limousine which suggested that he might now be employed in the family undertaking business as a driver.

They were going direct to the soap-box derby; but would have to walk part of the way, Harry warned them. All roads into Sandycombe had been sealed off at noon in anticipation of the ten thousand or so visitors the event was expected to attract.

As they journeyed between Michaelmas Cove and Sandycombe, Harry spoke anxiously of the difficulties he had encountered when testing his entry, *Hellfire*—there were so many spies about, he complained in an aggrieved voice—but at 2 A.M. that morning, *Hellfire* had done 68 m.p.h. along the narrow winding lanes in and around Sandycombe, at one point overtaking the beach buggy towing it. However, a research establishment, which had close ties with the aviation industry and therefore access (or so it was widely believed, Harry morosely told his guests) to a wind tunnel for test purposes, was rumoured to have clocked over 70 m.p.h. for its entry.

The event, which was in its fourth year, had attracted a record fifty entries. The mechanical engineering departments of several leading universities had entered vehicles this year, and the research and development sections of a number of large engineering firms from all over the country were also taking part for the first time. Several inquiries from abroad had given the organiser reason to hope that in the near future, perhaps even as early as next year, "International" could properly be included in the name of the event. For the present, though, the majority of entrants came from either Sandycombe itself or neighbouring towns and villages.

Harry parked on the outskirts of town and he and his guests walked with boisterous teenagers and straggling families of mothers and fathers and prancing young children the last half-mile to the start where a ramp roughly six metres high (which looked something like a ski-run) had been specially erected. (The ramp stood at the top of the town's main through road which Harry claimed had a drop of one hundred feet in ten times as many yards and wound its way down a hill, round a small park with an artificial lake and past the public lending library and the grammar school.) The race finished in the dead centre of town at The Coach and Four, a former coaching inn owned by the organiser of the event which was in aid of a local children's charity. As with the ramp at the start, the amount of cash raised reached new, dizzying heights each year. Approximately three metres had been added to the height of the ramp built for this year's race.

Harry left Mrs. Charles and Cyril behind a crowded rope barrier and disappeared into a garage at the rear of a service station. Most of the other competitors were already out with their vehicles. One of the race stewards was checking that no one was racing without brakes. It did not seem particularly relevant whether or not the brakes worked. (A man standing next to Cyril said it was a rule now that all entries must have brakes fitted. This was after one of last year's entrants finished up flying over the sea-front wall into the ocean—the tide, fortunately, was in at the time and no serious damage was done to man or vehicle.)

A man sitting in the neck of something which resembled a large aluminium jam funnel was yelling instructions to his wife (presumably) who was applying a lighted blowlamp to the metal hub of the vehicle's twenty-seven-inch bicycle wheels . . . Warming the ball-bearings, Cyril's well-informed friend thought.

There were a number of "flying bombs," something called *The Whoosh* which was mounted on an old Austin Morris motor car chassis and looked like a highly lethal hypodermic syringe, a good few traditional soap-boxes, several tanklike vehicles (the combined weight of which was over one and a half tons) and something which could have once been the nose-cone of a rocket ship.

An expectant hush fell over the crowd as Harry Brent made his appearance. Clearly, he was the star attraction and he rose to the occasion. He was kitted out in all white Formula One racing gear with "Grand Prix" printed in black on the back of his over-alls. The bright orange beach buggy in which he emerged from the garage was majestically towing a coffin on motor cycle wheels. The name of a life assurance company was emblazoned on the sides of the coffin under the name of the vehicle, which was boldly painted in psychedelic colours with long tongues of red, yellow and orange flame licking around it.

The beach buggy pulled up and the official brake-checker leaned over the coffin and said something to Harry who had hopped down and gone to meet him. Then, as the official turned away, Harry climbed into the coffin and raised what appeared to be the lever controlling a hand-brake and waved it cheerfully above his head. A loud roar of approval went up from the watching crowd.

A winch hauled heavier vehicles to the top of the ramp, but the electronically controlled timing was started automatically by the contestants themselves (who raced two at a time) as they came hurtling down the ramp and tripped the barriers at the bottom of it.

Mrs. Charles was never too sure who officially started the race; but all of a sudden, the first two contestants came swooping down the ramp and through the barriers and were then away, off down the hill with the crowd surging momentarily forward behind the barrier to watch them. It was difficult to sort out what was going on in the confusion which immediately followed since one of the contestants unexpectedly somersaulted to a halt when the metal pads fitted to the new revolutionary brakes he was trying out for the first time began to smoke and seized up.

A dish-shaped object entered and driven by Sandycombe's Church of England vicar won the race with the fastest time. Harry, despite a singularly spectacular take-off, never finished. Nor did the giant jam funnel which shared his run. Something went wrong with Harry's steering and he drove straight into the mouth of the funnel where *Hellfire* became firmly stuck. The Sandycombe Fire Brigade provided the cutting equipment to free Harry and his coffin from the funnel which was a total write-off.

At Harry's suggestion, the soap-box derby was not referred to again once he and his guests reached his home in case his older brother, who strongly disapproved of such frivolity, should return from his Sunday afternoon duty call on an elderly aunt and overhear their conversation.

Instead, Harry and Cyril talked animatedly about the old music hall days they had shared with only a minimum of regard for Mrs. Charles' presence until Harry's brother, Peter, finally joined them for tea. But not before Harry had performed his latest party piece; swallowed a long hank of cotton thread and then withdrew it slowly from his bared abdomen. He had assured his guests that there was "nothing to it" and had gone to fetch a needle and more thread to prove it when, mercifully, Peter Brent had arrived home and put an end to the macabre performance.

Peter Brent was nothing like his brother. He was much taller, balding, conventional to a fault—as was the bachelor brothers' meticulously neat home—and a rather dull conversationalist unless speaking of the dead. A friend of the Brent brothers with whom Cyril had been slightly acquainted had died recently, and Peter Brent spoke most eloquently on the subject, his contribution to the conversation concerning the manner of the deceased's passing being couched in such professionally sympathetic and practised terminology as to leave neither of his brother's guests in any doubt about his means of earning a livelihood.

It was Peter Brent who, towards the close of the visit, inquired —more out of politeness than real interest—what Mrs. Charles thought of Michaelmas Cove. A question that was destined never to be answered for it sparked off a heated altercation between the Brent brothers.

"Don't mention that place in my presence," said Harry, bridling effeminately. "You know how *ill* it makes me, Peter."

Harry's head suddenly swivelled round and his pale eyes bored like a gimlet into Mrs. Charles.

"Thoughtless and uncaring, that's what they called me," he told her. "Would you believe that?"

Mrs. Charles looked politely amazed. She was saved the need to comment by Peter Brent who said, "There you go again, Harry. You will overdramatise everything. There'd never have been any question of trouble if you'd been a little more moderate in your speech and hadn't been so theatrical about everything."

Harry was bristling with indignation. "Where's everybody's sense of adventure? Can't anybody see the funny side of anything any more?"

"Only a masochist would have a sense of humour about seeing his livelihood going up in smoke," said Peter Brent coldly.

Harry gave his brother a petulant look. "It was all your fault, anyway," he said. "You're the one who didn't want me buried alive any more. So all right; what do I do—?" He looked first at Mrs. Charles, then Cyril and finally at his brother. "I go for a cremation instead, and you and all those holier-than-thous over in Michaelmas Cove still aren't happy. Michael Thomas had no right to say those things about me. He's the last person who should throw stones at anyone."

This was obviously a strong bone of contention between the brothers and they glared angrily at one another.

"You really make me cross sometimes," said Peter Brent with a frown. "You've no right to talk about Michael Thomas like that. You've deliberately misunderstood his motives. It wasn't something personal between you and him. Half the people who live in Michaelmas Cove were affected by your reckless behaviour. Michael Thomas was only voicing their thoughts and feelings about the matter. It *was* thoughtless and uncaring of you not to take proper safety precautions before you set fire to yourself."

"*Me* misunderstand Michael Thomas? Oh, really?" Harry quivered with indignation and glared at his guests as if they had uttered the accusation and not his brother. "*Ho ho ho!* That's a laugh, I don't think. About as funny and thoughtful and caring as Mary O'Connell misunderstanding him that night in The Flying Dutchman and thinking she really was married to Albert May!"

" 'Del! Why, bless me!" exclaimed the old man. "And bless my soul . . . Cyril too. Come in, the pair of you, out of the cold. There's a chill wind tonight. You'll catch your death standing about out there like that!"

Beaming all over his face, the swami pumped Cyril's arm enthusiastically and then shoo'd his visitors into the sitting-room, leaving them there while he bustled out to the kitchen to get a bottle of what he called "the real McCoy" to celebrate the occasion.

"The real McCoy" proved to be an excellent French liqueur brandy . . . "Straight from the keg and no questions asked," admitted the swami, tapping the side of his nose and then, grinning from ear to ear, handing round the glasses.

"To old friends," he said, raising his glass.

"And the hermit," murmured Mrs. Charles.

The old man smiled happily at his visitors. "This *is* nice. I am pleased to see you both."

Mrs. Charles warmed her glass—a brandy balloon—in her cupped hands and said, "You might change your mind about that when you hear what I'd like you to do for me."

"For you, 'Del, anything," he said expansively. "Any favour you ask is yours. How can I help you?"

She smiled at him. "There's a slight possibility that I may want you to redeem yourself."

The swami looked at her uncomprehendingly, then widened his eyes at Cyril, as if hoping to find an explanation there.

"This really is like the good old times," observed Cyril vaguely. "Old friends coming together to help each other."

"Pearl Farrow," said Mrs. Charles, ignoring her brother who was obviously having another one of his conversations with himself. "I may need to ask you to challenge her authenticity again, Courtney."

His face fell. "You're joking, 'Del. Make a fool of myself all over again; is that what you're asking?"

"Ah, but this time, Courtney, you won't make a fool of yourself. This time *you'll* have looked at all the answers before the questions are asked."

"You mean—?" Shock showed in the swami's eyes. "I was right all along, wasn't I? Pearl Farrow *is* a fake!"

"Of course she is," said Mrs. Charles briskly. "I'm amazed that you ever doubted yourself."

"But—" The swami faltered, then frowned and shook his head wonderingly. "Well, bless me, bless my soul," he said slowly. "You've certainly led me up the garden path, 'Del. I never for one moment suspected that you doubted her genuineness."

"Only because your own convictions on the matter were so strong. If you'd asked me—which you didn't—I would've told you that she's a fake; and also that this was my main reason for coming here to Michaelmas Cove."

The swami looked astonished. "You came here to expose Pearl Farrow?"

She smiled faintly. "I'd like to think that I'm a tolerant person and would hope that I really do have the good, generous nature you once credited me with. However, I could never knowingly stand back and allow people to make capital out of their claim to be in possession of a gift which I've good reason to believe those persons do not and never will possess." The expression in the clairvoyante's eyes hardened. "It isn't even remotely likely that I would ever endorse what I know to be the illegitimate and fraudulent use of clairvoyance for the wholesale exploitation of the public at large. Nor would I ever wittingly allow someone to use clairvoyance as a smoke-screen to cover up that person's own personal involvement in blackmail and murder."

The swami frowned at her. "But how, 'Del? Pearl, poor child, isn't all there. And God forgive me for the way I keep on saying it, neither is her mother."

"Ronnie," said Cyril suddenly. "It's just come to me."

His sister and the swami looked at him blankly.

"That was his real Christian name," said Cyril. "Bridger's. I've been trying to think of it for days. Ronnie Bembridge, otherwise known as Bam Bridger."

Mrs. Charles looked at her brother for a moment; then, thoughtfully, at the swami. "Do you know him, Courtney? Bam Bridger? He ran a concert party for a time back in the fifties. Tall, nicely spoken, good-looking man."

"He's not now," said Cyril flatly as the swami shook his head.

Mrs. Charles looked at Cyril.

"The car accident," he explained. "You remember . . . I told you about it over the phone. Bridger was badly smashed up in a motorway pile-up a couple of years ago. His car caught on fire. He's lucky to be alive."

The clairvoyante sighed to herself. The burnt hamburger . . . So this was what that had all been about!

"Including his face, Cyril?" she inquired impassively, her patience with her brother born out of her total acceptance of him as he was.

"Yes," said Cyril and nodded. "Apparently it's a bit lopsided now and scarred where he had skin grafts and plastic surgery to rebuild it; and I understand he was very ill and in a lot of pain for some while afterwards. He got very depressed about it and had a breakdown. That chap I spoke to about Rita Jones said Bridger was convinced he was finished because he'd lost his looks."

"So there was a sinister scar-faced stranger wandering about on the cliffs the night Albert May died and Fr. Thomas had his accident," said Mrs. Charles meditatively.

"Bridger, you mean?" asked Cyril.

The swami looked bewildered. "Are you saying that Ida Claythorpe was right about Michael Thomas?" he asked Mrs. Charles. "He *was* pushed over the cliffs? This Bridger shoved him overboard?"

"No," said Mrs. Charles, shaking her head. "The man with the scarred face, Bam Bridger, I believe saved Fr. Thomas. But Mrs. Claythorpe was right that there was something odd about the accident. Fr. Thomas was pushed over the cliffs, and the man who was instrumental in effecting his rescue, Bam Bridger, saw who did it."

"Do you know who it was?" the swami asked her.

"I believe so," she replied.

The swami stared at her; and then, suddenly, a look of dismay crossed his face. "I don't know why I should feel this way, 'Del, but I've got a horrible feeling you're going to tell me it was either Mary Farrow or Pearl who pushed Michael Thomas overboard."

Mrs. Charles shook her head and smiled. "No, Courtney: it was neither of those two ladies; though heaven knows poor Mary Farrow had reason enough. She was telling the truth. She wasn't there. Neither was Pearl. But it was a woman. Peggy May pushed Fr. Thomas over the cliff-edge. To his death, she hoped."

CHAPTER 19

The swami switched his startled gaze from Mrs. Charles to her brother. Cyril, however, was miles away, back in Sandycombe reliving the pleasant afternoon he had spent in the company of his old friend Harry.

"Now, Courtney," the clairvoyante went on, "the time has come for us to cheat a little ourselves. I'm going to let you look at all the answers in much the same way that Pearl Farrow or rather her mother did."

He frowned at her.

"We are going to fight fire with fire, Courtney. Like Pearl Farrow, you too are going to become either the victim of a restless spirit who will reveal to you why the letters *AH* were scratched in the dirt near Doris Kemp's body; or you'll have a miraculous vision." She half-smiled. "Whichever you'd prefer. The choice is yours."

"Good Lord!" he exclaimed. "You mean I'm going to tell everybody—*the police?*—that those two letters stand for Adele Herrmann? Forgive me, but do you know what you're doing, 'Del?"

She gestured dismissively. "The police already know about Adele Herrmann: an inspector from Sandycombe spoke to me several days ago. Your friend Rita Jones kindly directed him to me," she told her brother, who wasn't listening. She looked back at the swami. "I think a phone call to begin with, don't you? One from you to the local newspaper which took such an interest in Pearl Farrow."

His eyes widened. "You want me to tell them that I've had the meaning of the letters *AH* revealed to me in some kind of vision?"

"Yes; and also that you'll make a public announcement and reveal all to them on—" She put a hand to her face and drummed her fingers thoughtfully on her cheek. "What say we make it the fourteenth day of next month? That," she said with a small smile, "should really put the cat among the pigeons."

"They'll just think I'm looking for some cheap publicity, 'Del," said the swami unhappily.

"Possibly. But they may also be just desperate enough for something to write about—as they were once before—that they'll publish your claim."

The swami's eyebrows rose. "Thinking I'm only bluffing and they'll make a fool of me again when the fourteenth comes round and I don't come up with the goods?" The old man paused, an anxious look in his eye. "Aren't the police going to wonder about this, 'Del, and come sniffing round my front doorstep just in case I'm not off my rocker and I really do have some vital information which they should know about?"

"They might. Personally, I doubt it. It's one of the advantages which people like you and I enjoy, Courtney," she said with a faint smile. "The police don't take us very seriously."

He grinned. "I've a feeling you're going to make 'em sit up and take notice all right."

Mrs. Charles thought of David Sayer. He was the only policeman—an ex-policeman at that—who really sat up and took notice of her (and even he was subject to lapses of prejudice!); but unfortunately, he wouldn't be around on this occasion to act as a buffer between her and his former colleagues.

"What's the significance of the fourteenth?" asked the swami.

Mrs. Charles said, "Doris Kemp told me that on the fourteenth of every month, Peggy May used to meet a certain gentleman friend; a sales representative, I now have reason to believe—" she gave her brother a look "—who came to Michaelmas Cove on business on that particular day each month."

The swami looked at Cyril. "This Bridger—the fellow you were talking about a few moments ago who had that road accident?"

Cyril did not reply. He had seen the look his sister had given him and decided that now was as good a time as any to go into one of his deep trances.

The swami nodded slowly, accepting Cyril's silence as a response in the affirmative. "All of a sudden," he said wryly, "it's not the police I'm worried about. This Bam Bridger is going to start getting very nervous about my miraculous visitation when (and if) he sees my reference to the fourteenth; the day when all will be revealed!"

"I would imagine so," said Mrs. Charles. "Does that bother you?"

"Only if he comes knocking on my front door asking me what's my game, and I've got to admit to him that I haven't the foggiest! I'd like to be able to give him one or two home truths about himself before he turns nasty on me." The old man's eyes widened meaningfully.

"We'll take care of that little matter right now," said the clairvoyante, smiling at him.

She opened her handbag and removed a small number of Tarot cards which were held together with a rubber band.

"What's this?" the swami asked.

"Peggy May's reading," Mrs. Charles replied. "The one I did for her twenty-five years ago."

"You can remember it?"

"Near enough," she said. "It was unusual, and for two reasons: the first because of what the cards revealed to me; and the second because I used a spread with which I was then experimenting. The Wheel of Fortune was removed by me from the combined Major Arcana and Lesser Arcana cards, and Peggy May (Baldwin as she was then) shuffled the other seventy-seven cards in the deck—mixing them up thoroughly so that some would be inverted—and dealt out seven of them, the first of those seven cards representing the hub of the Wheel of Fortune and being the card which would have the most dramatic influence on her future, and the remaining six standing as symbols for the six spokes of the wheel."

The swami nodded.

Mrs. Charles continued, "I chose that particular spread because Peggy had asked specifically to have her fortune told. The card crossing the Wheel of Fortune—the hub, remember—will be the key card."

"The Wheel of Fortune can be a difficult card to interpret," commented the swami. "Even with other cards around it as a guide to its meaning."

"Yes," agreed Mrs. Charles. She moved the drinks' tray aside and placed the Wheel of Fortune on the table. Then she held up the other seven cards and said, "Now these are the cards which, to the best of my recollection, Peggy Baldwin dealt out that night."

On top of the Wheel of Fortune, crossing it, the clairvoyante placed the first card, the Hermit—card No. IX in the Major Arcana. Then well to the left of the Wheel of Fortune she laid card No. II from the Major Arcana, the High Priestess. It was inverted. The next card to be laid down was another one from the Major Arcana, the Pope (upright), followed by the Lovers (upright), also from the Major Arcana. The Lovers fell immediately to the left of the Wheel of Fortune and the Hermit. Then, immediately to the right of the Wheel of Fortune and the key card, the clairvoyante placed another card from the Major Arcana, the Empress (upright) followed by the five of swords (upright) from the Lesser Arcana. The seventh and final card was from the Major Arcana. Card No. XV. The Devil (upright).

Mrs. Charles looked up at the swami who was gazing intently at the eight-card spread. He himself never suggested to his clients that they should mix up the cards so that some became inverted. An inverted symbolic picture card (i.e. with the picture upside-down to the reader) from the Major Arcana, for example, had a greatly altered meaning and he lacked Mrs. Charles' interpretive expertise. He doubted that many clairvoyants would be as skilled as she at reading the Tarot with all its various permutations.

"Well, Courtney," she said. "What would you make of that?"

He remained silent for quite some while. Then he said, "It's a very romantic reading . . . Feminine." He spoke as though he were being subjected to a test and was reluctant to commit himself too far with his answers until he had some definite indication as to whether or not he was on the right track.

"Yes," said the clairvoyante encouragingly.

He gained confidence. "Marriage is indicated," he said, tapping the Empress. "Yes, definitely marriage. But first," he went on, frowning at the Lovers, which was immediately to the left of the Wheel of Fortune and the key card, "a choice will have to be made. A difficult choice— When one relates it to the Wheel of Fortune, a choice which is going to affect Peggy's entire destiny."

He paused for a moment. Then, hesitantly: "The Hermit bothers me . . . its crossing the Wheel of Fortune. I would interpret that as a warning, a warning to exercise great caution. The Wheel of Fortune, however, overpowers it . . . That which is, was and always shall be—inevitability," he murmured. He paused. Then, thoughtfully: "While it is not the key card, the Wheel of Fortune dominates all else, particularly the High Priestess when that card is inverted as it is here. There is a secret here," he went on, nodding slowly, "a secret about which Peggy knows nothing . . . That would be my interpretation of the High Priestess and the Pope; the fact that the High Priestess is both inverted and influenced by the Wheel of Fortune indicating very strongly that this secret, when and if Peggy ever discovers what it is that has been deliberately concealed from her, will destroy her. Yes, and others too," he added, pointing to the five of swords. Hidden enemies will rise against her. But this will all be of her own doing. If she heeded the warning of the Hermit and withdrew, held a silent counsel— But no," he said, coming finally to the eighth card. "The Devil," he sighed. "The bearer of death, disaster and misery. That which is, was and always shall be . . . Nothing will stop the revolution of the wheel of fortune once Peggy sets it in motion by making her choice. Peggy will both destroy and be destroyed. *'All they that take the sword shall perish with the sword.'*"

He looked up at the clairvoyante. "Did you give this to Peggy straight or water it down a little?"

"Not just a little, quite considerably. As you've said, much, if not all of it was inevitable. Only she could alter the course of events which was to follow and it was too late for that: the wheel had already begun to turn, sealing her fate. Her husband-to-be, Albert May, had arrived at the place where we were partying that night to take her back home, thereby forcing her to make a choice between him and Bam Bridger, with whom she was then romantically involved, and fulfilling the first part of the prophecy of the Tarot."

"What did you tell her?" the old man asked.

"I told her that she was soon to marry, and that the marriage would be an extremely happy one; and then I warned her to be on her guard against a religious person, someone who had withdrawn from the outside world and held a secret which, should she discover it, would result in grief and great tragedy, both for herself and for those around her. She asked what I'd meant by a religious person, and I replied by saying that there were powerful occult influences in her reading—"

The swami interrupted her. "The High Priestess and the Pope."

"Yes; and that these occult influences, when one examined the overall picture, indicated a man of the church . . . some kind of recluse, I felt—a member of a closed order like a monk."

"Or a hermit?" suggested the swami.

Mrs. Charles shook her head. "That was never how I described him. Peggy called him that—twenty-five years later in her letter to me. She had recalled my warning and had interpreted it to suit her present circumstances; the hermit, according to her interpretation of those circumstances, being Fr. Michael Thomas."

"A monk of sorts," he said, nodding, "who belonged to a semi-secluded order and walked in the footsteps of the hermit of the local legend."

"Yes. He was the religious person with a secret. And I believe Peggy knew what that secret was when she sat down and wrote to me."

"Do you know what it was?"

"I made that discovery this afternoon. Fr. Thomas, in a mock wedding ceremony performed shortly before closing time late one night at The Flying Dutchman—a local public house which I understand is no longer in existence—married Mary Farrow, née O'Connell, to Albert May, a man with whom she, in common with most of the young girls living in Michaelmas Cove at the time, was deeply and hopelessly infatuated. Mary, incidentally, had been sent along to the public house by her father to fetch him a jug of ale. Unfortunately, Mary didn't realise that she was the victim of a cruel practical joke, and she took it all seriously. Albert May, egged on by his drinking companions, even spun her some colourfully romantic yarn about having to keep their marriage a secret for the time being, which she, being the type of girl she was—naïve and unsophisticated—swallowed whole. He, of course, had had a fair bit to drink that night, as had the young priest and the other three or four male witnesses to the mock wedding ceremony; and not surprisingly, the witnesses were later sworn to secrecy over the whole tragic affair. Albert May had his evil way (as they say) with her, and then when poor, naïve Mary discovered that she was pregnant, he refused to do the decent thing by her."

"Bless me," murmured the old man. "The poor girl. What a scandal!"

"Yes. But in the meanwhile, Mary had gone back to work as a parlourmaid on the Easterbrook estate. When, ultimately, she realised that a baby was on the way—and the joke that Fr. Thomas and Albert May and the others drinking at the public house that night had been having at her expense suddenly turned sour when Albert May refused to stand by her—she went to the only other person who could help her. Her elderly father.

"I don't know exactly when this happened," confessed the clairvoyante. "By that I mean how soon after Peggy Baldwin had walked out on Albert May and left Michaelmas Cove to pursue a dancing career, but I'm inclined to think that all of this must've occurred somewhere around the time that Mary's father suffered a stroke and died. I think the shock of her pregnancy and the revelation of a marriage that wasn't a marriage and never would be a marriage—and the shame of it all—killed him. But that's something only Doris Kemp's father—the village doctor— would've been likely to know; and possibly his other daughter

Phyllis, who helped him around the surgery. Aside from Mary Farrow, that is."

"What about Bridger?" Cyril suddenly interrupted them.

"Yes," said Mrs. Charles musingly. "Bam Bridger . . ." She paused to explain more fully the concert party organiser's former relationship with Peggy May. Then she went on:

"Bridger was hovering in the background the night I read the Tarot for Peggy and he, I believe, overheard every word we said to one another, including something Peggy remarked to me only a matter of a minute or so before Cyril interrupted us to tell her that someone—Albert May, we now know—was asking for her. I'd more or less finished the reading for her when she suddenly referred back to my warning and asked what I'd meant by powerful occult influences. It seemed to bother her. I started to explain that this phrase was professional jargon and merely the terminology I'd selected to express my belief in the threat that some kind of religious person would make to her in years to come. But before I could finish, she interrupted me and said, 'What about someone like you? It could be a clairvoyant, couldn't it?' At which point Cyril interrupted us, and Peggy rushed off. I never saw her again."

"You didn't warn her to watch out for the girl who was clairvoyant?" asked Cyril, surprised.

His sister shook her head. "Peggy obviously recalled some reference having been made to a clairvoyant; but over the years, she'd forgotten that it was she who'd brought someone like me, a clairvoyant, into the conversation. Then when Pearl Farrow and her vision suddenly burst in on her life, she again interpreted her recollection of the Tarot reading I'd done for her to suit her present circumstances. But only the threat of the hermit—the religious person I'd warned her about—was real. The girl who was clairvoyant was a figment of Peggy May's (and Bam Bridger's) imagination which they both later made into a reality to suit their own individual purposes. Neither one of them remembered that it was Peggy, not I, who had suggested that someone like myself might be a threat to her."

The swami frowned. "But why, 'Del? For what purpose would this Bridger want to create somebody who was clairvoyant?"

Mrs. Charles said, "My guess would be to frighten Peggy. And she was frightened; frightened enough to write to me for reassurance. The first part of my prediction had come to pass and she, naturally, believed that the remainder of it—the part concerning a clairvoyant, as suggested by her and overheard by Bam Bridger—would also come true. But it was too late for me to help her by correcting her mistake. By the time I received her letter, the wheel of fortune had moved on; it had almost completed its full revolution. Peggy May was dead—murdered, I believe—and there were only two spokes of the wheel still remaining to turn; the subsequent murder of Doris Kemp representing the fifth spoke of the wheel of fortune—"

The swami's eyebrows rose interrogatively. "And the sixth?" He glanced down at the cards, then looked back at Mrs. Charles. "The way I see it," he said slowly, "the wheel set off on its revolution with Bridger when he overheard your conversation with Peggy that night twenty-five years ago, and that's where it'll end. The full circle. Back with this Bridger." The old man widened his eyes at the clairvoyante. "That's if he's still about the place and hasn't had the good sense to put as much distance as he can between himself and Michaelmas Cove and Madame Adele Herrmann!"

Mrs. Charles smiled and shook her head. "No, Courtney: it all began with the hermit and his secret and that is where it will end. Look again at the cards, particularly at the Wheel of Fortune and the Devil, and tell me what you see."

The swami pored over the cards again, frowning. Then, abruptly, he raised his head and eyed Mrs. Charles curiously. "How did Peggy discover Michael Thomas' secret, and why did she try to kill him?"

"That," she replied, "is a long story."

"Well, in that case," he said, rising from his chair, "I think I'll pop the kettle on for a cup of tea."

CHAPTER 20

"The story began, of course, over twenty-five years ago when Mary O'Connell was seduced by Albert May," Mrs. Charles resumed when the swami returned with the tea-tray. "The final chapter of which was commenced the night Albert May died. The fourteenth of March last.

"It was on that particular night, March the fourteenth, that the scar-faced man whom Doris Kemp believed to have been meeting Peggy May secretly (Bam Bridger, as we've since discovered) became impatient. He was obviously aware that the end was very near for Albert May and so instead of going down to the caves to meet Peggy—which was their usual arrangement for the fourteenth of every month when business brought him to this part of the world—he went straight to the cottage; on his way there across the cliffs, running into Doris Kemp.

"Doris told me that Peggy was very upset about it—his going to the cottage—principally, I'd be inclined to think, because her husband's close friend and confessor, Fr. Michael Thomas, was there comforting him during his last moments. I also think there was a scene between Peggy and Bam Bridger, and she told him that she never wanted to see him again. Or words to that effect."

The swami interrupted Mrs. Charles while he passed her her tea. "A bit disconcerting, not to mention appalling bad taste," he remarked, "to have your lover waiting on the front doorstep ready to step into your husband's shoes when the poor devil hasn't quite stepped out of them yet himself."

"There was that point to it," she said. "However, I think there was something else as well. It'd been very flattering to have an old flame look her up; exciting to meet him secretly once every month during the long period of time that her husband was ill in bed; but things were different now. Come morning, her husband would be dead. She was about to become a free woman; one who was financially secure—extremely so, I believe."

"The old heave ho, eh?" said the swami.

"I would say so," she replied. "According to Doris Kemp, Peggy was still a very attractive woman and not yet in her fifties by my calculations. Not old by today's standards. There were going to be lots of men coming around, good-looking men, like there used to be when she was a young girl. She'd be able to pick and choose. It was all over between her and Bridger; and for him, that was history repeating itself. Peggy had thrown him over once before for another man. Never mind that Bridger had been a married man and had no right to expect her to dance to his tune. All he could see was that it was going to happen again. He left the cottage that night, no doubt severely shocked and upset about Peggy's abrupt change of attitude towards him."

The clairvoyante paused. Then, reflectively: "Only Bam Bridger could tell us what was in his thoughts that night as he wandered about the cliffs brooding over Peggy's rejection of him. Taking into account his facial disfigurement—and the mental breakdown Cyril told us Bridger suffered after the accident when he despaired for his lost good looks—one wouldn't find it too difficult to imagine how he must've felt. Rightly or wrongly he would've almost certainly blamed his physical appearance for his present predicament and quite understandably been overwhelmed with self-pity and despair. But then the wheel of fortune turned on its axis again, and in so doing permitted Bridger, I believe, to become the silent, unobserved witness to a quite extraordinary scene. An old priest was coming along the cliff-path, away from the cottage which Bridger had himself left only a short while earlier."

The swami nodded and said, "Michael Thomas."

"Yes; and coming up behind him was Peggy whom I suspect had overheard certain instructions which her dying husband had given to his priest and friend concerning Mary Farrow."

"Ah," said the old man, nodding slowly. "That was how Peggy learned the hermit's secret."

Mrs. Charles nodded and said, "And she didn't like what she'd heard."

The swami made a small face. "A nasty shock to discover that your husband and Mary Farrow had been keeping that secret from you all those years."

The clairvoyante frowned. "No, I don't think it was that so much. I strongly suspect that Albert May had made secret provision for Mary Farrow and his child, Pearl, which Fr. Thomas was to see reached them. Albert couldn't acknowledge Mary and Pearl in his will. It would've been unthinkable to subject his wife and Mary and Pearl to all the gossip and scandal after all those years—"

"You think there was a lump sum for the Farrows kept either somewhere in the cottage or placed with Michael Thomas and entrusted into his care?" asked the swami.

"In view of subsequent events, yes," said Mrs. Charles. "I'm quite certain there was. Peggy and the priest argued, I think quite violently, on the cliffs. It might've even been the continuation of an argument which started at the cottage after she'd overheard her husband and Fr. Thomas talking together.

"But I believe Fr. Thomas stood firm," the clairvoyante went on. "The money was going to Mary Farrow and Pearl in accordance with Albert's wishes. And that left Peggy with no choice. There was only one way she could stop the bequest reaching its intended destination (and I think we can safely assume that with Pearl being the way she is, so totally dependant on her mother, it was a fairly sizeable legacy). It would be my guess that Fr. Thomas was carrying the money meant for the Farrows on him when he left the cottage that night, probably in some kind of parcel or package; and Peggy, having caught up with him on the cliff-top near Jupiter's Lookout, managed to relieve him of it."

Mrs. Charles paused and widened her eyes. "I've seen Fr. Thomas: he isn't a robust man; and as would seem to be fairly common knowledge, he'd had a fair bit to drink that night and would've undoubtedly been quite unsteady on his legs, not to mention severely emotionally distressed over the passing of his old friend. He would've been no match for an enraged female; a woman with an unreasoning, inflamed desire to keep what she considered rightfully to be hers. To find out, as I'm quite sure Peggy did that night, that your husband had been supporting another woman and their child right under your nose for all those years would come as a terrible shock to any woman; but more so to one who, according to her best friend Doris, was close with money."

The swami said, "Albert finally did the right thing by Mary and stepped into the breach when her husband was killed in the farm accident?" He nodded his head thoughtfully. "It would certainly make some sense of what happened to Michael Thomas on the cliffs that night. That's if you're right and Peggy did try to ring down the final curtain on the poor old boy once she'd got her hands on the bundle of lolly intended for the Farrows." He paused and smiled wryly. "This Bridger fellow's eyes must've nearly popped out of his head when he saw Peggy shove a priest overboard."

"I should imagine so. I also think their argument, which Bridger definitely overheard, gave him quite considerable pause for thought."

The swami nodded his agreement. "The possibilities for blackmail being uppermost on his mind," he said. "Though I don't know so much," he added doubtfully. "I'd think again, very carefully, about blackmailing someone who'd ruthlessly push an elderly gentleman of the cloth (hopefully) to his death. I can't see that kind of person having too many scruples or much of a conscience. It's a situation that would have to be handled with the utmost care and caution; that's if I, the blackmailer, wanted to live out my allotted threescore and ten!"

"Exactly," said the clairvoyante. "And Bridger would've had no illusions about that, either. However, as the shock of what he'd heard and seen wore off, he suddenly remembered my prophecy for Peggy of twenty-five years ago concerning a man of the church—"

There was a quickening of interest in the swami's eyes. "And then he made his mistake."

Mrs. Charles smiled faintly. "Yes. In his excitement over one minute having nothing, and then the next having a loaded gun thrust into his hands, he mistakenly thought I'd also warned Peggy about a clairvoyant."

"And so he created one specially for her benefit," said the swami with a slow smile. "And who better than Pearl Farrow for that neat final twist of the knife? However, for his plan (the one I can now see him beginning to formulate in his head) to have its best effect, it would be better if the priest were alive so that the threat of the religious person, as prophesied by you, was still there hanging over her head."

He looked at the clairvoyante questioningly and she nodded. "And luck, for want of a better word," she said, "was with him all the way. Fr. Thomas had fallen onto a ledge and was still alive; not seriously hurt."

The swami interrupted her with a slow nod. "And so he went to Mary Farrow with what you must admit was a very daring plan to introduce her mentally retarded daughter to the world as a clairvoyante—a visionary—and thereby terrify Peggy into parting with not just the money that Fr. Thomas had had entrusted into his care for the Farrows, but with anything else that Bridger and Mary Farrow could lay their hands on. Bridger would even the score for her having tossed him aside and get paid for his trouble. And Mary Farrow . . . Well, who could blame poor, frustrated Mary for trying to get what should've been hers anyway? Michael Thomas wasn't likely to make a song and dance about what had happened and broadcast to everyone Mary Farrow's shame and the disgraceful part he'd played in it. It wouldn't have been what any of them wanted; Michael Thomas, Albert May or Mary Farrow. Not after having kept their secret so well and for so long. Bridger's proposition would've been Mary's only hope of getting what was due to her without disgracing herself and her child."

The old man gazed absently into his empty teacup. Then, after a moment, he poured himself another cup of tea and one for Cyril when he pushed his cup forward.

"So," the swami said, "Mary already knew that Michael Thomas had gone over the cliffs when she called in a neighbour to sit with Pearl while she came down into the village to fetch the doctor." He looked up, wide-eyed. "It must have given her a few anxious moments when she discovered that the doctor was out on a call and she had to wait around for her return. Mary would know better than most how a minute wasted in Michael Thomas' kind of accident can be the difference between life and death." He paused while he drank from his cup. Then: "I must say she played her part well . . . Tricking the doctor—and everybody else—the way she did. Though she was lucky there . . . That the doctor was fairly new to the village. Somebody like old Dr. Kemp wouldn't have been so easily hoodwinked." He frowned. "I assume that eventually—that is once Bridger had successfully established Pearl as a clairvoyante in everyone's eyes (the poor, gullible public's and Peggy May's)—Pearl would experience a further remarkable psychic encounter with the spirit world; in this instance principally for Peggy May's benefit concerning the manner in which Fr. Thomas came to fall overboard."

The clairvoyante nodded. "That eventuality came to pass, I would think, shortly before Peggy wrote to me. Possibly even something that same day, if we're to read anything significant into the date of her letter. June fourteen. Bridger would've been in the village that day . . . Though in her letter, of course, Peggy mentioned only that the mother of the girl who was clairvoyant had spoken to her recently. No doubt for the sole purpose of acquainting Peggy with the fact that Pearl had started to have some very odd visions about Peggy and Fr. Thomas and an argument up on the cliffs over money which should've come to the Farrows. One can imagine how very frightened Peggy must've been. She would've been at a pretty low ebb anyway; what with her plans for Michael Thomas going awry and his still being alive and knowing that she'd tried to kill him. And now somebody else knew it too. The girl who was clairvoyant. And who'd question anything that Pearl Farrow was reputed to have said? No one. Not after her previous success in saving Fr. Thomas' life. But there was still some fight left in Peggy. She had one last hope. Me. And so she sat down and wrote her letter; hoping, one would suppose, that I'd be able to resolve her terrible predicament in some way for her."

"But—" The swami looked puzzled. "Her death. It doesn't fit. Suicide, yes. She was pushed too far by Bridger and Mary Farrow and she cracked under the strain." He narrowed his eyes at Mrs. Charles. "My ears weren't playing tricks on me: you did say she was murdered?"

"It's there in the cards, Courtney," she said, inclining her head at them.

He studied them again. "With hindsight; yes, perhaps I can see it. The possibility of a violent death, anyway. But surely—" he frowned at the cards "—if the girl who was clairvoyant never existed and was created merely as an afterthought, a convenience, and the hermit—or religious person—was the only real threat to Peggy, as you foresaw, then she was murdered by—" He raised his head, a startled look in his eyes. Then, looking back at the cards: "No, it can't be. You can't possibly be so sure about something as horrible as that."

"But I am sure, Courtney," she said. "Perhaps not so sure to begin with as I was the moment you told me that Doris Kemp had been stabbed to death with an unusual knife—one used by a fisherman, you said."

"Rita Jones," said Cyril abruptly and frowned.

Mrs. Charles and the swami looked at him.

"What about her?" asked his sister.

"Where does she fit in?"

Mrs. Charles said, "You answered that question yourself when you said Bridger still kept in touch with all his girls—the ones who used to be on his books when he was a theatrical agent—and gave them advice and help when they were down on their luck. Rita Jones told me she was out of a job and having difficulty finding work. She also said she was waiting around for a friend who was due to join her the following day, the fourteenth."

"Bridger?" asked Cyril.

"It had to be him, though I didn't realise it at the time, of course," his sister confessed. "Then when Bridger finally turned up, she mentioned that she'd met me in Sandycombe the previous day. And from that moment on, as far as Rita Jones was concerned, it was a simple matter of a favour for a favour. Bridger would help her if she'd help him by going to the police with certain information about Adele Herrmann. No doubt in the hope that this would scare me off."

"He doesn't know you very well, does he?" remarked Cyril.

"No," she said. "That was his second mistake."

CHAPTER 21

It was shortly before eleven P.M. when the clairvoyante and her brother returned to The Mermaid. They exchanged whispered good-nights and then went their separate ways.

Mrs. Charles had just entered her room and was removing her cloak when she heard a light footfall in the corridor outside her door. She paused and listened intently. Everything went quiet. Then there was a rustling sound and a long white envelope shot across the carpet almost to her feet. Leaving it for the moment where it was, she crossed quickly to the door, opened it quietly and looked out. Liza Murdoch turned the corner at the top of the corridor and disappeared.

Thoughtfully, Mrs. Charles gently closed the door, then picked up the envelope and opened it. There was nothing written on the outside of the envelope. The short, handwritten message she found inside it ran as follows.

If you don't want the police to find out about you and Peggy May and what you were doing at her cottage on Tuesday when Doris Kemp was there, be at Jupiter's Lookout at midnight. Come alone. You are being watched.

The note wasn't signed.

The clairvoyante looked up. This was something she hadn't expected. Bridger had panicked. It was the first really stupid move he'd made. *Or been forced to make; was that it?*

A chill closed round the clairvoyante. Something, or someone, had forced Bridger's hand. Scared him off. And it had nothing to do with anything she'd discovered about him and Mary Farrow since coming to Michaelmas Cove. She was no real threat to him. Not yet. He just had to sit tight and wait it out. Or sit tight and wait until she pushed him into making a move. That would've been the smart thing to do; and what she'd expected to happen. She frowned slightly. Maybe Bridger had had enough and thought it best now to get out. While he still could . . .

She folded the note and slipped it back into the envelope; sighed. Poor Courtney. His redemption was never to be. *"That which is, was and always shall be,"* she could hear him saying. The sixth spoke in the wheel, the final turn, the full circle. It had come much sooner than she had anticipated.

It was bitterly cold. The cliff-paths were treacherously slippery but reasonably well lighted by the mournful sodium lamps which were dotted at lengthy intervals apart across the cliffs like sad and lonesome sentinels.

As Mrs. Charles reached the path which would take her to Jupiter's Lookout, she paused and looked back at the twinkling lights of the village; the dominant red glow of the brash neon sign on the George Hotel farther down the street from The Mermaid. Then she turned and walked steadily on. Her thoughts went back to Peggy May's Tarot reading and the card which had inevitably brought the clairvoyante herself to what she knew could prove to be a very dangerous moment in her own life. In her mind's eye, she pictured the wheel of fortune; watched its helpless victims ascending the right-hand side of the wheel and then begin to descend it on the left, tumbling one after the other to their fate with the turning of its axis . . . Fr. Thomas, Peggy May, Doris Kemp and then, finally—

A small noise on the clairvoyante's left brought her to a sudden halt. She stood perfectly still and listened, searching the melancholy shadows with her eyes.

There was someone coming up behind her, following her progress step by step along the winding, pebbly path. Out of the corner of her eye she glimpsed the outline of a long overcoat, its collar turned up to meet the hat which was pulled well down on the wearer's head.

She pushed on. Drawing level with the lamppost a short distance back from the bench near Jupiter's Lookout, she paused again and turned around. Whoever had been following her was no longer there.

Shivering a little, she drew her cloak warmly around her, then went up to the bench and sat down. It was a few minutes to midnight.

The moon came out from behind a clump of cloud and lay in a cold white band across the shiny black ocean. It was a cheerless sight. Sad and depressing, thought the clairvoyante.

She heard a sound, but did not investigate it immediately. Waiting for as long as she dared, she then turned her head slowly and rose unhurriedly to face the hulking shadow standing watchfully by the large boulder to her right. The moon momentarily disappeared. As it came out again, the clairvoyante started to move.

"Stay right where you are!" commanded a gruff voice.

"I'd rather not," said Mrs. Charles pleasantly. "If you wouldn't mind. That guard-rail doesn't look at all safe to me, and it's a rather long drop down there, as Peggy May discovered when you sent her hurtling to her death."

There was no response from the shadow.

Mrs. Charles laughed softly. "Poor Bam Bridger— It's really quite extraordinary that as a witness to the attempt which Peggy May made on the life of Fr. Thomas, he recognised the danger he was in from her, but failed to realise that he was in even greater danger from you, Mrs. Farrow—a woman whose psychotic hatred of men turned with the passing of the years into a murderous contempt for all mankind."

The shadow started a little and then moved a step or two nearer. Mrs. Charles could not see Mary Farrow's face, but she knew she was being watched with intense malevolence.

"It must be a great consolation to you, Mrs. Farrow," the clairvoyante quietly continued, "to know that you, after suffering so cruelly and for so long from the heartless, unprincipled trick which a man once played on you, were able to turn the tables and exact your revenge. Not on Albert May, the man who had so disgraced you and was the cause of all your grief and misery—it wasn't in your best interests for any harm ever to come to him by your hand—but on the woman he married instead of you, and her lover Bam Bridger. Or Ronnie Bembridge. Whichever name you know him by.

"Where is he now, Mrs. Farrow? Lying at the bottom of the cliffs? Did you send him tumbling to his death too? You've finished with him, haven't you? Always a fairly shrewd and clever showman who knew how to bring on the crowds, he demonstrated to you how you could punish the whole wide world for your years of suffering and humiliation, didn't he? He isolated your own great weakness and pandered to it by showing you how to make fools of everybody, and how you could make much more money than either one of you had ever envisaged by blackmailing Peggy May, the widow of the man who'd so shamed and disgraced you all those years ago. You wanted full retribution for your pain and suffering; for the anguish of the lifelong burden of a severely mentally handicapped daughter; and Bam Bridger, the showman, gave you the know-how and the means of getting it."

Mary Farrow moved slowly out of the shadows. What little that was visible of her face beneath the man's grey felt hat she was wearing had been turned a sickly purplish colour by the yellow light shining down from the lamp. "I hated them," she said in a low, hard voice. "All of them. Everyone in the village. All my life they've poked fun at me and laughed at me. Well, now it's my turn. We'll see who laughs last and longest. Peggy May, Doris—"

"Was it you who listened through the mail-slot while Doris and I were at Peggy's cottage?" interrupted the clairvoyante. Her eyes widened questioningly. "Bridger? Or was it his friend, Rita Jones?"

"Ronnie only ever came up here once," snapped Mary Farrow.

"Yes, I know . . . The night Albert May died. Doris told me."

"What a pity she's dead," Mary Farrow sneered. "The police might've taken some notice of her. You'd be lucky if they gave you the time of day. They've had enough of you ouija board bashers. We all have."

"Dear me," said the clairvoyante. "That sounds ominously to me as if Michaelmas Cove is about to have another fake suicide. More visions?" She paused and shook her head. "No, Mrs. Farrow. There's a greater force at work here; a force much more powerful than you or I. Inevitability. The wheel of fortune has turned, completed its full revolution, and in so doing it has cast you and Bam Bridger aside as it has cast off all the others before you; the people whose destinies became tragically linked with Peggy May's."

"Mumbo-jumbo!" snarled Mary Farrow. "Ronnie said you were one for the words."

"In that way he's been quite clever himself," remarked the clairvoyante impassively.

"Greedy," said Mary Farrow. Her voice was cold; bitter. "Like all men. Never satisfied. Thirty per cent; that was what he wanted. Thirty per cent of everything we took from the shrine and the magazine and television deals he'd got set up for us. He thought Pearl and I were going to see him sitting pretty for the rest of his life. Some girl in the village was making a nuisance of herself around him and he was getting fed up with her and reckoned it was time he was moving on. He'd got her in the family way, she said. She wanted him to marry her, but he wasn't having any of that. He was going to run out on her and leave her high and dry. Couldn't have cared less that she was going to have to face her parents and friends and live with her shame all alone . . . Even said it wasn't true; she was making it all up; imagining things. Well, I showed him. I showed him you can't use people like that." She paused. Then, in an aside: "Oh no, he's not using Pearl and me. He's ended up with thirty per cent of nothing. No one gets anything for free from Mary Farrow any more."

"The worm had finally turned."

"Yes, the worm *had* turned. Nobody, *but nobody*, was going to get in my way. Especially you. Peggy warned me that she'd sent for someone. She wouldn't tell me who it was, but Ronnie guessed it'd be you. You were a long time in the coming, but you finally turned up, and I was ready for you. I spotted you going past my cottage late Tuesday morning and I followed you. Ronnie'd told me what you looked like so I was fairly sure I had the right person. I couldn't get any sense out of that stupid woman who was trailing around everywhere after him hoping he'd get her a job—she was mooning about there on the bench waiting for him to finish his round down in the village, and I knew she'd spoken to you in Sandycombe the day before—so I went on up to the Mays' cottage and heard for myself all I wanted to know."

"Was that why you killed Doris?" the clairvoyante asked. "Because she'd talked to me? Or was it because she was Peggy May's best friend? How you must've hated her for that. And she would've always been something of a threat to you, anyway, wouldn't she? Her sister, Phyllis, knew about you and Pearl and Albert May, didn't she? Phyllis Trout had kept your secret, but that mightn't have always been the case. Somehow, someday, Doris might've stumbled on the sad truth about you and Peggy's husband and started to wonder if her friend really had committed suicide after all. Doris had most of the pieces to the puzzle; and with that one final vital piece of information, she might've sat down and put the whole picture together and seen you for the pitiful fake you really are. So you killed her. But sadly, Mrs. Farrow, it rarely ends there. You'd seen the proof of that long before you killed her. Whereas in the beginning there was only one antagonist, Peggy, then there were two, Doris and me. And so it would go on, with the number of people against you multiplying every time you cut one of us down. Only you can't fight the whole world, much as you might like to. You couldn't go on forever faking suicides and leaving the initials of innocent people's names scratched in the dirt near the bodies of your other victims . . ."

"Not just one for the words, are you?" said Mary Farrow contemptuously. "Clever with it. Too clever by half. Just like Ronnie thought he was. He couldn't see he was signing his death warrant by coming back here specially tonight and writing that note to you for me and then getting his ex-wife—that painted hussy who runs The Mermaid—to deliver it to you. No stomach!" she snorted disgustedly. "Like all men when they've got to face up to the unpleasant consequences of their actions. He was only too happy to leave it to me to take care of you; just like I had to take care of his girl-friend Peggy when she started to become difficult and said she wasn't going to pay up any more. She met me up here and told me she was going to write to *her friend* again." Mary Farrow simpered in an attempt at mimicking Peggy May's voice. "She was going to tell *her friend* exactly what had been going on . . . And now, Madame Herrmann, or Mrs. Charles—whatever you call yourself!—having poked your long nose in where it wasn't wanted and made that discovery for yourself—"

"*'Del, 'Del!*" a thin voice quavered on the chill night air.

"Up here, Cyril," responded Mrs. Charles in a loud, clear voice. "My brother," she explained to Mary Farrow.

The clairvoyante watched her stiffen.

"Ronnie never said anything to me about a brother."

"Then that's something else he forgot with the passing of the years," said the clairvoyante cryptically. "And I rather fancy, Mrs. Farrow," she went on quietly after a slight pause, "that my brother won't be alone."

"The police?" There was a shocked silence. Mary Farrow seemed to shrink. She cringed back into the black shadows like a badly wounded animal. "Pearl," she said. Her voice had an oddly distant quality to it. "She needs her mother, you know. She's not a strong child. It's her chest; that's why I've got to keep her indoors so much. It's spoilt all her chances of a normal life, you understand."

Cyril panted up to his sister. "We went the wrong way. I thought you said the caves. It was only when we found Bridger lying down there on one of the paths that I remembered we were supposed to follow you up here."

"What about Bridger?" she asked.

"Dead," said Cyril. "Broken neck. Looks like he fell from one of the paths higher up. Or jumped. I daresay that's what everybody's meant to think . . . That's if he was the one who wrote that note to you. We're supposed to think he met you up here at midnight, like it said in the note, then he killed you and committed suicide. It must've happened as he was on his way down to the caves to wait while Mrs. Farrow took care of you. I'd say she sneaked up behind him and gave him a hefty shove sideways; caught him completely unawares. It was just like you said it'd be. She sorted him out once and for all!"

Cyril's voice took on a complaining note.

"I had the devil's own job convincing the police—that inspector-bloke you told me to contact—that I wasn't a head case when I told him you'd come up here to meet the person who'd murdered Doris Kemp. It wasn't until I said he'd probably find the murder weapon he's looking for in some kind of shoemaker's—cobbler's—tool-box at the Farrows' cottage that he started to take any real notice of me."

Mary Farrow was standing near the guard-rail gazing out to sea.

"That her?" he whispered.

Mrs. Charles nodded.

"She looks more like a man than a woman," he observed.

Yes, thought Royal, who had finally caught up with the more spritely Cyril Forbes and overheard the comment. He had thought the same thing about Mary Farrow.

Royal turned to Mrs. Charles. "Madame . . . Mrs. Charles," he said breathlessly. "I think you've got quite a lot of explaining to do."

"My pleasure, Inspector," she said and smiled. "Whenever you're ready."

A flash of annoyance went through him. "You don't seem to appreciate the very grave risk you've taken in coming here alone tonight, madame."

"Risk, Inspector?" The clairvoyante sounded quite surprised. "I've never been in any real danger."

His irritation with her grew. "And how, may I ask, do you make that out?"

"The cards, Inspector. The Tarot? It wasn't in the reading."

He looked at her; gave up in disgust.

He went over to Mary Farrow and placed a hand on her arm.   M4

She turned, stared hopelessly into his face, then looked past him at Mrs. Charles.

"Who told you my secret?" she asked in a dull voice. "It wasn't Phyllis Trout . . . I know you went to see her; Fr. Thomas told me. But she'd never break her promise . . ."

"A man scorned," the clairvoyante quietly replied, recalling the manner in which Harry Brent had made the startling disclosure about Albert May and Mary Farrow. "In the right set of circumstances, Mrs. Farrow, his wrath can be no less than a woman's."

Royal looked from one woman to the other. He assumed they knew what they were talking about. He certainly didn't.

Epilogue

Mrs. Charles shook hands with Courtney Harrington, who had accompanied the clairvoyante and her bother to the bus-stop and was waiting now to see them off to Sandycombe on the first leg of their journey back home.

"You'll be back for the trial?" asked the swami, and she nodded.

"I'm pleased you've decided to stay on in Michaelmas Cove," she said. "Things didn't go quite the way we planned them, but in time I think you'll find that the end result will be the same. People soon forget and remember only what they want to remember; usually that which causes them the least embarrassment."

The swami sighed. He seemed depressed. "I've been stopped twice in the street this morning—once by a complete stranger—and told by both people that they'd agreed with me all along and knew right from the beginning that there was something fishy about Pearl Farrow." He sighed again and shook his head sadly. "It certainly is a funny old world."

The clairvoyante looked back over her shoulder at the smooth sea; the cliffs; the white-washed fishermen's cottages; the clear blue sky; the black-faced gulls wheeling and calling to one another.

"Yes," she said quietly.

Mignon Warner was born in Australia, but now lives in England with her husband, whom she assists in the invention, design, and manufacture of magic apparatus. She spends most of her free time pursuing her interest in psychic research and the occult. Her previous novels about the clairvoyante Mrs. Charles include *Death in Time, The Tarot Murders,* and *A Medium for Murder.*

93 96 04
11 1 5

1